和全球做生意
必備簡報英語

Essential English for Presentations

發 行 人　鄭俊琪

總 編 輯　陳豫弘

執行主編　林詩嘉

中文編輯　游凰慈・鍾明頤・林怡君

英文編輯　Steven Melo

英文錄音　Mike Tennant・Ashley Smith・Courtney Aldrich

藝術總監　李尚竹

美術編輯　黃薪宸

封面設計　黃薪宸

介面設計　陳淑珍

技術總監　李志純

程式設計　李志純・郭曉琪

執行製作　翁稚緹

出版發行　希伯崙股份有限公司

　　　　　105 台北市松山區八德路三段 32 號 12 樓

　　　　　電話：(02) 2578-7838

　　　　　傳真：(02) 2578-5800

　　　　　電子郵件：service@liveabc.com

法律顧問　朋博法律事務所

印　　刷　禹利電子分色有限公司

出版日期　2020 年 9 月　初版一刷

定　　價　320 元

和全球做生意
必備簡報英語

Essential English for Presentations

英語數位學習第一品牌

CONTENTS

編者的話

快速學會英語簡報<u>關鍵用語</u>，
打造一場成功的<u>英語簡報</u>！

在高度國際化的商場上，相信不少人都曾遇過得全程用英語做簡報的情況。然而，許多人的共同經驗常常是詞不達意、支支吾吾甚或不知所云。這樣的窘境，足以讓人對於用英語做簡報感到戰戰兢兢。一場精彩且成功的商務簡報並不是看著投影片內容照本宣科，而是得妥善利用圖表和條列的重點，輔以清晰有條理的話術，將統整過的資訊傳達給聽眾。為了幫助有心充實英語簡報能力，並期許能和客戶開啟合作契機的商務人士，本書規畫了 **6 大主題共 24 種情境**的簡報英語會話。

簡報前的準備	帶你熟悉簡報的核心要素、製作要領和基本話術。
介紹公司	你能學會用英語介紹企業沿革、組織架構、相關部門以及重要幹部。
爭取客戶	你能一次備足合作提案的簡報話術，成功爭取到客戶。
介紹產品	涵蓋新品發表、促銷宣傳、參展籌備等相關主題的實用簡報英語。
公司運作	包含說明年度企畫、報告發展策略、發表年度展望以及重大訊息記者會等實用內容。
營運表現	你能輕鬆掌握年度預算、業績報告和圖表數據所必備的簡報話術。

精彩內容

圖解詞彙 迅速掌握各單元的關鍵用語。

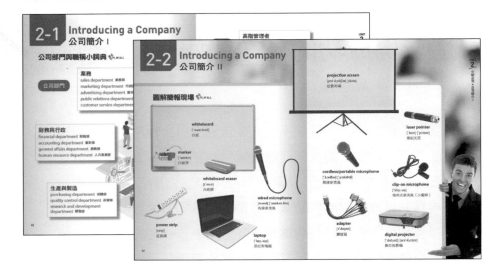

主題實用句 收錄各單元的必備重點句。

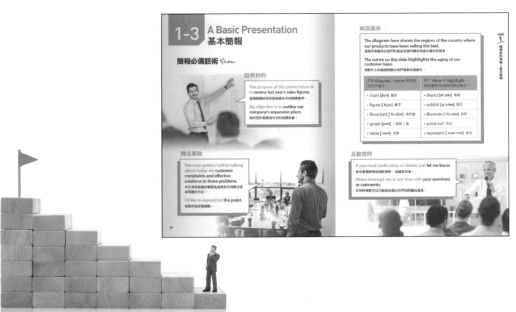

影音會話 精選 24 種簡報實況，搭配真人影片，讓你能實際演練。

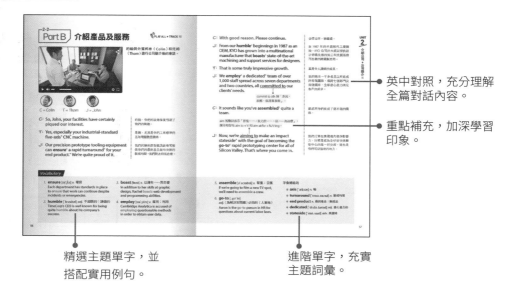

英中對照，充分理解全篇對話內容。

重點補充，加深學習印象。

精選主題單字，並搭配實用例句。

進階單字，充實主題詞彙。

重點筆記 詳細說明各單元所出現的實用語，並搭配例句。

延伸學習 補充各單元的相關資訊，讓你的學習臻於完整。

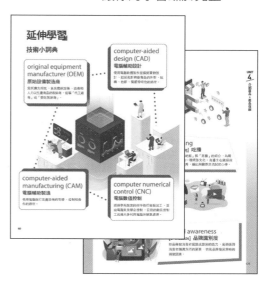

點讀筆功能介紹

認識點讀筆

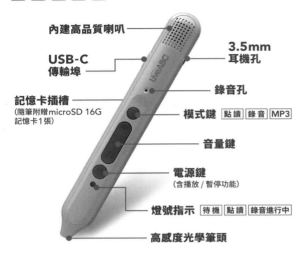

- 內建高品質喇叭
- USB-C 傳輸埠
- 記憶卡插槽
  （隨筆附贈microSD 16G 記憶卡1張）
- 3.5mm 耳機孔
- 錄音孔
- 模式鍵 點讀 錄音 MP3
- 音量鍵
- 電源鍵（含播放 / 暫停功能）
- 燈號指示 待機 點讀 錄音進行中
- 高感度光學筆頭

三大特色 | 16GB 記憶卡 | USB Type-C | 可充電鋰電池

四大功能

- ◆ 點讀發音
- ◆ 錄音發音
- ◆ MP3 播放
- ◆ 英漢字典

 高科技光學點讀筆頭

 內建高品質喇叭

 支援USB 檔案傳輸

 點讀/錄音 MP3/字典 四機一體

尺寸	151 x 20 x19 mm
重量	36±2g（內含鋰電池）
記憶體	含 16GB microSD 記憶卡
電源	鋰電池 (500mAH)
配件	USB 傳輸線 (Type-C Cable)、使用說明書、錄音卡 / 音樂卡 / 字典卡、microSD 記憶卡（已安裝）

安裝點讀音檔

1. 使用前請先確認 LiveABC 點讀筆是否已完成音檔安裝

Step 1
將點讀筆接上 USB 傳輸線並插入電腦連接埠。

Step 2
開啟點讀筆資料夾後，點選進入「Book」資料夾。

Step 3
確認本書音檔（書名 .ECM）是否已存在於資料夾內。

2. 若尚未安裝音檔，可依照下列 2 種方式下載點讀音檔 (.ECM) 並安裝

方法 1 請至 LiveABC 官方網站 (www.liveabc.com) 搜尋本書，進入介紹頁面後，即可下載點讀音檔。完成解壓縮檔案之後，再將點讀音檔 (.ECM) 複製到點讀筆「BOOK」的資料夾裡即可。

方法 2 安裝本書電腦互動學習軟體，（點選管理及執行欄位），如圖示下載點讀音檔，完成解壓縮檔案之後，再將點讀音檔 (.ECM) 複製到點讀筆「BOOK」的資料夾裡即可。

請至此處下載點讀音檔，並儲存至電腦桌面。

開始使用點讀筆

點 PLAY ALL 圖示，即可聽到本頁對話及單字內容。

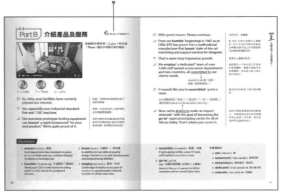

Step 1

1. 將 LiveABC 光學筆頭指向本書封面圖示。

2. 聽到「Here We Go!」語音後即完成連結。

◆ 每本書可點讀的內容依該書編輯規畫為準

搭配功能卡片使用

錄音功能 請搭配錄音卡使用

模式切換：點選 RECORD & PLAY 錄音卡，聽到「Recording Mode」表示已切換至錄音模式。

開始錄音：點選 ⊙，聽到「Start Recording」開始錄音。

停止錄音：點選 ⊙，聽到「Stop Recording」停止錄音。

播放錄音：點選 ▶，播放最近一次之錄音。

刪除錄音：刪除最近一次錄音內容，請點選 🗑。
（錄音檔存於資料夾「\recording\meeting\」）

MP3 功能 請搭配音樂卡使用

模式切換：點選 MUSIC PLAYER 音樂卡，並聽到「MP3 Mode」表示已切換至 MP3 模式。

開始播放：點選 ▶，開始播放 MP3 音檔。

新增 / 刪除：請至點讀筆資料夾位置「\music\」新增、刪除 MP3 音檔。

英漢字典功能 請搭配字典功能版使用

模式切換：點選 Dictionary ON，聽到「Dictionary on」表示已切換至字典模式。

單字查詢：依序點選單字拼字，完成後按 ↵，即朗讀字彙的英語發音和中文語意。

關閉功能：使用完畢點選 Dictionary OFF，即可回到點讀模式。

更多點讀筆使用說明請掃描 QRcode

UNIT
1
Presentation
Preparation
簡報前的準備

1-1 Presentation Core Concepts
簡報基本要素

簡報 8 步驟與核心概念 PLAY ALL

1 Subject 主題

2 Purpose 目的

3 Data 資料

4 Slides 投影片

What is my subject?
我該訂定什麼主題？

- Do thorough research　充分進行研究
- Know your audience　了解你的聽眾

簡報達人小提醒
首先，研究簡報的主題、要點並擬定大綱。接著，了解目標聽眾為何，以及他們對該主題的認識程度與可能需要或者會感到有興趣的資訊。

Practice
練習

Opening
開場白

Elaborate
鋪陳

Q & A
問答

Why am I making this presentation?
為什麼我要做這份簡報？

- Provide information　提供資訊
- Inspire action　激發行動

簡報達人小提醒

簡報時要注意音量、肢體語言和臉部表情。如果你展現對簡報主題及內容的熱忱，你的聽眾也會感受到你的投入與熱情。

What information should I share?
我應該涵蓋那些資料？

- Need-to-know vs. Nice-to-know
  「務必知道的」和「知道了也不錯的」
- Flow structure　流程結構

簡報達人小提醒

將簡報內容分成三至五個重點。過多的要點反而容易分散聽眾的注意力（可將細節歸到次要項目）。在陳述某個要點前，先扼要敘述；在結束一論點並要進入下一要點時亦可提示聽眾。

1-1
Part A 討論簡報要素

亨利（Henry）將進行一場簡報，艾力克斯（Alex）提供他一些做出完美簡報的建議……

A = Alex   H = Henry

A: Hello, Henry. How's next week's presentation coming along?

H: Hi, Alex. Actually, not too great. I'm not sure how to get started. Any advice?

A: Well, there are three core areas to **concentrate**[1] on: content, design, and delivery. For the first part, you need to do your research, organize your points, and then create an **outline**.[2]

哈囉，亨利。下週的簡報進行得如何？

嗨，艾力克斯。說實在的，不怎麼好。我不確定要怎麼著手。有什麼建議嗎？

嗯，有三個核心範圍要注意：內容、設計以及表達。關於第一部分，你得做研究，組織你的要點，而後擬定大綱。

Vocabulary

1. **concentrate** [ˈkɑnsənˌtret]
   v. 全神貫注（+on）
   With so much noise from the street, Cassie was unable to concentrate on her studies.

2. **outline** [ˈautˌlaɪn] n. 大綱；概要
   All students must submit outlines of their research projects by the end of the week.

3. **visualization** [ˌvɪʒəwələˈzeʃən]
   n. 形象化；想像
   The basketball player believed that visualization helped him improve his shooting abilities almost as much as actually practicing.

H： OK. Then I guess the design part is deciding on the software and graphics I use.

A： Exactly. Delivery is also key. Many people **clam up** when speaking in public, so **visualization**[3] can help.

H： You mean I should imagine myself delivering the presentation?

A： Not just any presentation, but the perfect presentation! Good delivery also helps **ensure**[4] your audience gets your point, and that it **effects**[5] the change you're aiming for.

H： Anything else?

A： Well, you know about the three P's, right?

H： No, what are they?

A： First is "purpose." What is your subject and why will it benefit the target group? Next is "people." How much do the listeners know and what information do they need? Finally, "place" is important. **Identify**[6] the room and equipment you'll be using.

好。那麼我猜設計的部分是決定我要使用的軟體和圖像。

沒錯。表達也很重要。許多人在公眾場合演講時會開不了口，因此形象化會有幫助。

你是說我該想像自己做簡報的情形嗎？

不只是一般簡報，而是完美的簡報！好的表達方式也有助於確保聽眾了解你的觀點，而這會帶來你所期望的改變。

還有其他的嗎？

嗯，你知道所謂的 3P 吧？

不知道，是什麼呢？

第一是「目的」。你的主題是什麼以及它為何對目標群眾有所助益？接著是「對象」。聽眾知道多少以及他們需要什麼資訊？最後，「地點」也有其重要性。確認你將會使用的場地和設備。

---

4. **ensure** [ɪnˋʃʊr] v. 確保
   To ensure that she would receive a promotion, Ally worked late every day.

5. **effect** [ɪˋfɛkt] v. 實現；造成
   Raising salaries can effect large changes in staff performance.

6. **identify** [aɪˋdɛntəˏfaɪ] v. 確認
   Spencer had problems identifying the key points of the speaker's presentation.

討論簡報資料

艾力克斯接著向亨利傳授整理簡報
資料和擬定大綱的訣竅……

H = Henry　　A = Alex

H: So how do I start researching my content?

A: Make a list of the information you need, where you're going to get it, and how long it will take.

H: So if I need figures, for example, I'd contact Sales.

A: Yep. And for info on how our product benefits the client, you'd go to Marketing. Also, put your content into "need-to-know" and "nice-to-know" categories.

那麼我要如何開始研究內容？

列出你所需資訊的清單，你要從哪裡取得這些資訊以及這會花你多少時間。

舉例來説，如果我需要數據，我就去聯絡業務部。

沒錯，而關於公司產品如何受惠於客戶的資料，你就要去行銷部。此外，將你的簡報內容分為「務必知道的」和「知道了也不錯的」兩個類別。

Vocabulary

1. **crucial** [ˈkruʃəl] *adj.* 關鍵性的
   David played a crucial role in the event; without him, it wouldn't have been a success.

2. **handy** [ˈhændi] *adj.* 實用的
   Bob bought a handy filing unit for the office.

3. **informed** [ɪnˈfɔrmd] *adj.* 有見識的；了解情況的
   My coworker always keeps me informed about the latest stock market developments.

H： The first category is the **crucial**[1] details, I suppose; the kind of stuff I should include on slides. What are the "nice-to-know"?

A： Those are just **handy**[2] facts and figures that will make you seem more **informed**[3] and help you deal with questions from your audience.

H： How will I know exactly what they need to know?

A： That can be **tricky**,[4] as it can change depending on the audience. You should avoid **one-size-fits-all**[5] solutions. Tailor your presentation to your target group.

H： All right. Any tips for **drafting**[6] the outline?

A： Decide on your style, and organize the content into three to five main points. Any more and you may lose your listeners' attention. The details can be subpoints.

H： Thanks for all of your advice! You've been a great help.

A： Not a problem.

我猜第一個類別是關鍵細節，像是我應該放在投影片裡的東西。「知道了也不錯的」類別是什麼呢？

就是一些有用的詳細資料，能讓自己看起來更有見地，並幫助你處理聽眾的問題。

我要怎麼確切知道哪些是他們得知道的資訊？

那可能有點棘手，因為取決於聽眾而會有所改變。你應該避免一體適用的解決方案。要為你的目標群眾量身打造簡報。

好的。草擬大綱有什麼訣竅呢？

決定簡報風格，然後將內容分成三至五個要點。再多下去你可能會分散聽眾的注意力。細節可歸到次要項目。

感謝你的這些建議！你幫了很大的忙。

別客氣。

---

4. **tricky** [ˋtrɪkɪ] *adj.* 棘手的
Jeff's new DVD player is a little tricky to operate.

5. **one-size-fits-all** [wʌnˋsaɪzˏfɪtsˋɔl] *adj.* 一體適用的
The European Union is often criticized for having one-size-fits-all policies.

6. **draft** [dræft] *v.* 起草；草擬
Max drafted a new version of the proposal.

重點筆記

1. come along 有進展；進步

說明	come along 在此表示「發展；進步」，另外亦常指「出現；發生」。

- The plans for the big event are coming along fine.
  該大型活動的計畫進行得很順利。
- Robert knew that the chance to work with a famous film director didn't come along often.
  羅伯特知道和名導演合作的機會不常有。

2. clam up（突然）沉默不語

說明	此語比喻人像蛤蜊（clam）緊閉蚌殼般「閉住嘴巴；沉默不語」。

- Dean is outgoing among friends but clams up around people he doesn't know well.
  迪恩和朋友在一起時很外向，但和不熟的人在一起時就變得很安靜。

3. sub- 次於；在⋯⋯以下；低於

說明	字首 sub- 有「次於；在⋯⋯以下；低於」等意思，常見應用如下： sub + culture 文化 = subculture 次文化 prime 主要的 = subprime 次級的 zero 零度的 = subzero 零下的 total 總計 = subtotal 小計

- Subprime lending was a major factor in the recent global financial crisis.
  次級借貸是近期全球金融風暴的一項主因。

延伸學習

簡報好用句

製作簡報時，清楚介紹自家公司的背景和商品能為客戶帶來好印象。
快來看看有哪些實用句吧！

背景

Our company was founded in **2003** in **California**.
我們公司於 2003 年成立於加州。

規模

Our factory is **about 18,000 square feet**.
我們的工廠大約為一萬八千平方英呎。

Tall Glass Co. operates 57 plants in **the U.S.** and 100 plants worldwide.
拓爾玻璃公司在美國有五十七座廠房，全球則有一百座工廠。

產能

We have a production capacity of **2,000 units a week**.
我們每週有兩千組的產量。

WeeTots Company recently increased its production capacity by **four times**.
威塔茲公司近來增加了四倍產能。

產品特色

This smartly designed cell phone is perfect for **people on the go**.
這款智慧型設計的手機非常適合在外奔波的人士。

This device was made with the needs of **busy mothers in mind**.
這個裝置是為了滿足忙碌母親們的需求而製造的。

This computer beats out its competitors in terms of **size and processing power**.
這台電腦在尺寸與資料處理能力方面擊敗了其他競爭者。

1-2 Presentation Slides
商務簡報製作

簡報製作要領 🖋 PLAY ALL

1. Have one concept per slide

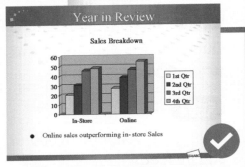

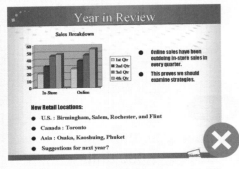

Problem: Too many concepts on one slide

問題：一張投影片有太多概念

Solution: Spread information over more than one slide

解決方法：將資訊分置於多張投影片

2. Keep phrasing consistent

Year in Review

- Despite difficulties in Q1, which have been attributed to causes beyond our control, we have managed to meet our goal of having 118 stores open worldwide.
- Sales have grown significantly in the Asian market, are falling a bit in Europe, and will likely decrease in North America for the rest of the quarter.

Year in Review

- We have met goal to have 118 stores open worldwide.
- Sales have increased in Asia and decreased in Europe and North America.

Problem: Complicated wording and mixed tenses, phrases, or clauses

問題：措辭複雜且時態、詞組或句構不一致

Solution: Simple wording and parallel structures

解決方法：簡單的措辭與平行的結構

3. Make data into graphics

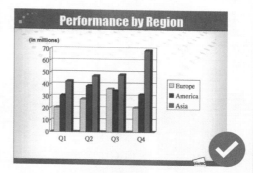

Performance by Region

Region	Q1	Q2	Q3	Q4
Europe	20.4	27.4	36	20.4
America	30.6	38.6	34.6	31.6
Asia	42.5	46.9	48	68.6

(in millions)

Problem: Hard to identify any change or difference

問題：難以分辨任何變化或差別

Solution: Easy to visualize information in charts or graphs

解決方法：以圖表呈現可方便資訊的視覺化

圖表類別大不同

圖表雖能讓簡報達事半功倍之效，但使用不當卻可能造成聽眾的困擾。以下是常見的圖表類型與其適用情境：

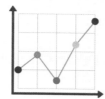

line graph 折線圖

多用來呈現總銷售量（total sales）、價格（price）、營收（revenue）和費用支出（expenditure）等的趨勢或走向。

bar chart 長條圖

常用來比較同性質（nature）但不同項目（category）、範圍（range）或時期（period of time）的數據差異。

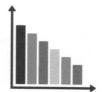

pie chart 圓餅圖

用來顯示某項目和整體比例（percentage）的關係。

Part A 討論投影片的製作

亨利（Henry）向艾力克斯（Alex）請教如何製作專業的簡報投影片⋯⋯

H = Henry　　A = Alex

H: Hi, Alex. Have you got a minute to answer a couple of questions about my PowerPoint presentation?

A: Sure. **Fire away**.

H: Well, firstly, I'm wondering how many main ideas I should have on each slide.

A: You should have just one key concept per slide. You can add some extra bullet points expanding the idea but don't **overload**[1] the slides. It will **overwhelm**[2] your audience.

H: OK, anything else?

嗨，艾力克斯。你有空回答和我的 PowerPoint 簡報有關的一些問題嗎？

當然。你說吧。

嗯，首先，我想知道每張投影片我應該放幾個重點。

每張投影片你只應該放一個主要概念。你可以加些額外的要點來闡明這個概念，但切記別過量。這會讓你的聽眾吃不消。

好，還有其他的嗎？

Vocabulary

1. **overload** [͵ovəˋlod] *v.* 過量；使負荷過多
Piper overloaded her essay with so many facts and figures that it was difficult to actually read.

2. **overwhel** [͵ovəˋwɛlm] *v.* 使不知所措
The new intern was overwhelmed by all the things she had to do.

A： Make sure your phrasing is **consistent**.[3] Use nouns and verbs, and keep them in the same tense. Your audience will appreciate this **parallel**[4] structure. Try sticking to the eight by eight rule, too: no more than eight lines per slide, with eight words to a line.

H： I see. How many slides should I have in total?

A： Well, that depends on the length of the presentation, but aim to go through one or two slides a minute. Bear in mind your style as a presenter. If you're a talker who is likely to go into detail about each point, you'll need fewer slides.

H： How about graphics? I want to use them, but I've seen some terrible presentations where I couldn't understand what the tables and graphs meant.

A： That's always a danger, so it's crucial to make sure they are clear and not too <u>busy</u>.

於此指「繁瑣的；雜亂的」。

確定你的用詞一致。使用名詞和動詞並保持相同的時態。你的聽眾會理解這樣的平行結構。也試著遵守八乘八規則：每張投影片不超過八行，每行則不超過八個字。

了解。我總共該做幾張投影片呢？

嗯，那取決於簡報的長度，但你要以一分鐘簡報一或兩張投影片為目標。時時記住你是什麼類型的簡報者。如果你是個可能會詳加介紹每個要點的能言善道者，你需要的投影片就會比較少。

那圖像呢？我想使用圖像，但我看過一些可怕的簡報，當中的表格和圖表令我一頭霧水。

總是有風險在，所以一定要確保圖表清晰且避免過於繁雜。

---

3. **consistent** [kənˋsɪstənt] *adj.* 一致的；始終如一的

Murray was praised by the department director for his consistent performance.

4. **parallel** [ˋpɛrəˌlɛl] *adj.* 平行的

The two streets are parallel.

Part B 準備和演練

艾力克斯向亨利解釋簡報前的注意事項，包括聲調和語調等……

H = Henry   A = Alex

H： OK, that's the slideshow covered. I'm still pretty nervous, though. Any suggestions for preparing?

A： Well, having the basics in place to start with will help you relax. It goes without saying that you need to be dressed for success.

H： My Sunday best, eh?

A： Yep. Turn up well in advance and ensure everything is in order, like the seating arrangements, the lighting, and the equipment. If your presentation is right after lunch or late afternoon, you might want to try some icebreakers to keep your audience engaged.[1]

投影片的部分都沒問題了。不過我還是很緊張。有任何準備的建議嗎？

嗯，從搞定基本項目開始能幫助你放鬆。無庸置疑地，穿著得體是成功的基礎。

我最好的服裝是吧？

是啊。及早到場並確保每件事都準備就緒，像是座位安排、燈光以及設備。如果你的簡報緊接在午餐後或傍晚時進行，你或許可試試一些活絡氣氛的東西來保持聽眾的注意力。

Vocabulary

1. **engage** [ɪnˋgedʒ] v. 吸引住；使感興趣
   The key to effective speaking is to engage your listeners at all times.

2. **monotonous** [məˋnɑtənəs] adj. 單調乏味的
   Katie was sick of the monotonous duties she had to complete every day at her job.

H: Good idea. I was planning a couple of brief activities anyway for a change of pace.

好主意。我本來就打算進行幾個簡短的活動來改變簡報的步調。

A: Good. But be flexible. If something isn't working, try and adapt.

很好。但要有彈性。如果活動無效，要試著調整。

H: Speaking of adapting, I'm a bit worried about not being able to vary my tone enough. I don't want to sound **monotonous**.[2]

說到調整，我有點擔心無法充分地變換自己的語氣。我不希望自己聽起來單調乏味。

A: Practice **accentuating**[3] important words and avoid the standard newsreader-type patterns, you know, emphasizing syllables regularly regardless of their significance.

練習強調重要的字眼並避免制式的新聞播報模式，你曉得的，就是習慣性強調每個音節，不管其重要性。

H: How about my pitch? I don't want my voice going up and down or cracking in mid-sentence.

那我的聲調呢？我不希望自己的聲音忽高忽低或講到一半時破音。

意同 in the middle of a sentence or utterance，即「句子的中間；話說到一半」。

A: Try repeating "uh-huh" to yourself. Seriously. Professional speakers have discovered this shows you your **optimum**[4] speaking pitch. Got it?

試著對自己複述「呃哼」。不蓋你。專業演說者發現這能展現你的最佳說話聲調。懂嗎？

H: Uh-huh!

呃哼！

---

3. **accentuate** [ɪkˋsɛntʃəˏwet]
   v. 強調；使突出

   The highlights in the model's hair accentuated the color of her eyes.

4. **optimum** [ˋɑptəməm]
   adj. 最理想的

   Right now, the pool is at the optimum temperature. It feels great!

重點筆記

1. *fire away* 請說

說明	原本形容如連珠炮式地說話，後引申指「開始發問；儘管問」，常用在會話中請別人開始說話或提問。

- Whenever you're ready to ask your questions, fire away.
  你準備好問題時，就儘管問吧。

2. *Sunday best* 最好的服裝

說明	在美國和其他西方國家，人們星期天去教堂時通常會穿得比較正式，因此 Sunday best 用來指稱一個人最漂亮的衣服，也就是適合婚禮等特殊場合的正式服裝。

- Employees at the Internet firm were allowed to dress casually on most days, but they were required to wear their Sunday best for important meetings.
  這家網路公司的員工在多數的日子裡都能穿得很休閒，但參加重要會議時，他們被要求得穿正式服裝。

3. *well in advance* 及早

說明	in advance 指「提早；預先；事前」，前面加上 well 有加強的作用，表示「大大提前；及早」。

- The doctor asked that patients notify her well in advance if they needed to cancel appointments.
  該醫師要求她的病人，若需要取消預約得及早通知她。

延伸學習

「簡報」熟能生巧！

做簡報往往令許多人感到非常緊張，但只要有充分的準備及演練，
你也可以成為縱橫職場的簡報達人！

Arrive early and dress appropriately.
提前抵達，穿著得宜。

Ensure everything is in order.
確保一切井然有序。

Adjust your tone and pitch.
調整你的語氣和聲調。

Check the equipment you need.
檢查你所需的設備。

Make sure your PowerPoint slides can run on the computer.
確認你的簡報檔能在電腦上運作。

簡報預備檢核表

簡報前，記得確認下列項目都準備到位。

✅ computer and projector　電腦和投影機

✅ lighting and temperature　燈光和溫度

✅ supply of water and handouts　供水和講義

✅ dress and appearance　衣著和外表

✅ microphone or headset　麥克風或頭戴式耳機

1-3 A Basic Presentation
基本簡報

簡報必備話術  PLAY ALL

說明目的

The purpose of this presentation is to **review last year's sales figures.**
這場簡報的目的是檢視去年的銷售數字。

My objective is to **outline our company's expansion plans.**
我的目的是概述公司的拓展計畫。

陳述要點

The main points I will be talking about today are **customer complaints and effective solutions to these problems.**
今天我將談論的要點為客訴和有效解決這些問題的方法。

I'd like to expand on **this point.**
我會詳述這個論點。

解說圖表

The **diagram** here **shows** the regions of the country where our products have been selling the best.
這張示意圖秀出我們的產品在國內哪些地區有最好的銷量。

The **curve** on this slide **highlights** the aging of our customer base.
投影片上的曲線突顯出我們客群的高齡化。

可和 diagram、curve 替換使用的字還有：	除了 show 和 highlight，解說圖表可搭配的動詞還有：
• chart [tʃɑrt] 圖表	• depict [dɪˋpɪkt] 描述
• figure [ˋfɪgjə] 數字	• exhibit [ɪgˋzɪbət] 顯示
• flowchart [ˋfloˏtʃɑrt] 流程圖	• illustrate [ˋɪləˏstret] 說明
• graph [græf] （曲線）圖	• point out 指出
• table [ˋtebəl] 表格	• represent [ˏrɛprɪˋzɛnt] 意味

互動提問

If you need clarification or details, just **let me know.**
若有需要解釋或細節說明，請讓我知道。

Please interrupt me at any time with **your questions or comments.**
任何時候都可以打斷我並提出你們的問題或意見。

Part A 簡報開場

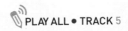

亨利（Henry）向公司的董事會委員
簡報最近幾季的銷售成績……

H = Henry　　B1/B2 = Board Member One/Two

H： I'd like to begin by thanking you all for being here today. Don't worry. I'll be sure to get you all out of here before lunch.

B1： Well, this presentation is off to a good start already.

H： The purpose of my presentation is to review the company's sales performance during the last two quarters. I'll begin by talking about total sales, then **touch on**[1] **regional**[2] sales, and finally discuss market share.

首先，我要感謝各位今天的出席。別擔心。我一定會讓大家在午餐前離開這裡。

嗯，這場簡報已經有個不錯的開始了。

我的簡報目的是檢視公司過去兩季的銷售成績. 我會從談論總銷售量開始，然後觸及區域銷量，最後則討論市占率。

Vocabulary

1. **touch on sth** 提及某事物
   Holly didn't think the professor touched on any of the important points in his lecture.

2. **regional** [ˈridʒən!] *adj.* 區域性的
   I need to contact the regional office in Hong Kong on a weekly basis.

3. **internal** [ɪnˈtɜn!] *adj.* 內部的
   Employees use their internal message system to communicate in the office.

B2: Didn't we get an **internal**[3] e-mail about this already?

關於這點我們不是已收到內部電子郵件了嗎？

H: Indeed, you did. But in this presentation I'll go into further detail and answer any questions you may have, so feel free to **interrupt**[4] me at any time.

沒錯，各位是收到了。但在這場簡報中，我將深入細節並回答你們可能有的任何問題，所以各位隨時都可以打斷我。

B2: OK. When do we get to see some facts and figures?

好。我們何時能看到正確的數據資料？

H: Right now. Let's take a look at this line graph showing sales over the last six months. You can see a sharp increase here in the weeks leading up to summer.

就是現在。我們來看看這張顯示過去六個月銷量的折線圖。各位能看到夏季前的幾個星期，銷量急遽攀升。

B1: Immediately followed by an even bigger decrease.

隨後緊接著出現更大的跌幅。

H: Right. The **spike**[5] in sales during the vacation period is **predictable**.[6] However, as you can see in the graph, sales reached new lows in the first week of September.

是的。暑假期間的銷量暴衝是可預期的。然而，各位可從圖表看到，九月第一週的銷量達到新低點。

B1: Well, it's clear as day, people. We need to increase our post-summer sales.

嗯，這很清楚了，各位。我們勢必得增加公司的夏末銷量。

---

4. **interrupt** [ˌɪntəˈrʌpt]
   v. 打斷（他人的談話）

   It was not polite of Kelly to interrupt the boss while he was speaking.

5. **spike** [spaɪk] *n.* （價格、利率等）驟增

   A spike in interest rates caused problems with the property market.

6. **predictable** [prɪˈdɪktəbəl]
   adj. 可預料的

   The poor Q2 sales for the firm led to a predictable drop in share prices.

Part B 回答提問

亨利繼續向董事委員們說明簡報中
的內容並回答其提問⋯⋯

H = Henry   B2/B1 = Board Member One/Two

H: It's not all bad news. If I can move on to the next part of my presentation, you'll see a slide with a bar graph showing sales performance in different regions.

B2: This includes all of our sales territories, right?

H: That's right. As you can see, the East Coast **did a great job** these past two quarters. The increase from last year's sales is **obvious**.[1]

B1: Whoa! What happened to the West Coast? It's way down at the bottom.

也不全然是壞消息。在我簡報的下個部分，各位將看到投影片中的長條圖顯示不同區域的銷售成績。

這包括我們所有的銷售區域，對吧？

沒錯。如各位所見，東岸過去兩季表現非常優異。與去年的銷售額相比，增長明顯。

哇！西岸是怎麼回事？銷量一路跌到谷底。

Vocabulary

1. **obvious** [ˈɑbvɪəs] *adj.* 明顯的
   It was obvious that Julie could not lift the heavy sofa.

2. **significant** [sɪgˈnɪfəkənt] *adj.* 重要的；顯著的
   There was significant interest from several parties when the company put itself up for sale.

H： Sales were disappointing there. However, you can see that in the rest of the regions, sales were up across the board.

那裡的銷量令人失望。不過，各位可看到，在其餘的區域，銷量是全面成長的。

B2： How are we looking in comparison to our competitors?

和我們的競爭者相比，我們的表現如何？

H： I'll answer that with the next slide. As you can see in this pie chart, we hold a **significant**[2] section of the market. However, our share is still smaller than our biggest **rival**'s.[3]

我會在下張投影片回答這個問題。各位可在這張圓餅圖中看到，我們在市場中占有一席之地。然而，我們的市占率仍小幅落後我們最大的競爭者。

B1： But haven't we **gained**[4] market share since last year?

可是我們的市占率不是自去年就增加了嗎？

H： Yes, we've been growing slowly but steadily. On that note, I'd like to bring my presentation to an end. And, as promised, it is right before noon.

是的，我們的成長緩慢卻很穩定。說到這兒，我想我的簡報就到此結束。一如先前允諾各位的，正好在中午前結束。

B2： He's a man of his word.

他是個說話算話的人。

H： I'm available to answer any questions you have, now or during lunch.

不論是現在或午餐時間，我都可以回答各位的任何問題。

---

3. **rival** [ˈraɪvəl] *n.* 競爭對手；敵手
The two teams have always been rivals.

4. **gain** [gen] *v.* 得到；獲得
Jeff gained valuable experience while working overseas.

重點筆記

 PLAY ALL

1. *off to a good start* 有好的開始

說明	此片語形容以非常有利或建設性的方式展開某事物,意即「有好的開始」。

- Francis and Tim have worked together well before, so their new project is already off to a good start.
  法蘭西斯和提姆之前就合作無間,所以他們的新專案已經有好的開始了。

2. *go into detail* 深入細節

說明	detail 指「細節;詳情;枝節」,go into detail 即形容對某件事情交代細節部分,也就是「詳細說明」的意思。

- Vanessa went into detail about why she thought her business plan ultimately failed.
  凡妮莎詳述她認為自己的生意最終失敗的原因。

3. *facts and figures* 正確的數據資料

說明	facts and figures 為押頭韻的成對詞,形容有關特定情況或主題的基本細節、數字等資訊。

- Please don't give me all the extra details. I just need the facts and figures.
  請不要給我所有的額外細節。我只需要精確的資料就好。

4. *lead up to* 就在……之前

說明	此語表示「(時間)臨近……」,用法為「時間 + lead up to + 某事」,指「臨近某事前的時間」。

- Marilyn was very excited in the days leading up to her birthday.
  瑪莉蓮在生日到來的前幾天感到非常興奮。

5. (as) clear as day 顯而易見的

說明	此片語應用了句型 as + adj. + as + N.，描述「跟某事物一樣的……」，(as) clear as day 字面意思是「跟白天一樣清楚」，即比喻「顯而易見的」。

- Jack's true feelings about the merger were as clear as day.
  傑克對於併購案的真實感受顯而易見。

6. do a great job 表現非常優異

說明	此用法源自 do a good job「做得出色」，job 指「事情；工作」。good 可替換成其他形容詞，如對話中的 great。

- Jeff didn't do a great job writing the report, so it will have to be rewritten.
  傑夫沒有把報告寫得很好，所以必須要重寫。

7. across the board 全面地

說明	在美國賽馬場合中，每匹賽馬都有專屬的計分板（board），上面有賭其獲得第一、第二或第三名的下注紀錄。若某匹賽馬的得獎希望濃厚，三項都下注，可大大提升中獎機率。這種全面下注的賭法遂引申指「全面地」。

- Thanks to profit sharing, extra earnings are distributed equally to employees across the board.
  多虧利潤共享，多餘的盈利可平均分配給所有員工。

8. in comparison to 和……相比

說明	comparison 為動詞 compare「比較」的名詞形式，in comparison to/with 可表示「與……相較」。

- The cost of living in Taipei is very reasonable in comparison to London.
  和倫敦相比，台北的物價合理多了。

9. *slowly but steadily* 緩慢卻很穩定

說明	此副詞片語形容緩慢地、漸進地做某事，但取得的結果會是明確的，類似用法為 slowly but surely。

- Slowly but steadily, the company is becoming successful again.
  緩慢而穩定地，該公司再次邁向成功。

10. *on that note* 說到那個

說明	note 一般可指「注意；注目；筆記；音符」，on that note 的意思則是「說到那個」，語意近似 speaking of that。

- I'd like to thank you for coming to this event, and on that note, let me hand the floor over to tonight's guest speaker.
  我要感謝大家蒞臨此活動，說到這兒，讓我將時間交給今晚的演講嘉賓。

11. *a man of his word* 守信用的人；說話算話的人

說明	word 在此表示「諾言」。若主詞為女性，則要說 a woman of her word。

- Lyle is a man of his word, so I believe him when he says he can do something.
  萊爾是個說話算話的人，所以當他說他辦得到某件事時，我是相信他的。

延伸學習

回答提問好用句

開放提問時可以這樣說

Please feel free to ask questions.
請儘管提問。

If you would like me to elaborate on any point, I would be happy to do so.
如果你們想要我詳加解釋任何論點，我很樂意説明。

回應問題時可以這樣說

【直接回應】

A good question. I think we should look at Graph A one more time.
這是個好問題。我想我們應該再看一次 A 圖表。

I'm glad you've asked that question. As I said earlier, this has a lot to do with our annual budget.
很高興你提出這個問題。如我先前所説的，這和我們的年度預算息息相關。

【間接回應】

I'll come back to this question later in my presentation.
稍後在簡報中，我會再回到這個問題。

We'll be examining this point in more detail later.
我們稍後會再深入探討這點。

UNIT
2

Company
Presentations
介紹公司

Introducing a Company
公司簡介 I

公司部門與職稱小詞典 🎧 PLAY ALL

公司部門

業務
sales department 業務部
marketing department 行銷部
advertising department 廣告部
public relations department 公關部
customer service department 客服部

財務與行政
financial department 財務部
accounting department 會計部
general affairs department 總務部
human resource department 人力資源部

生產與製造
purchasing department 採購部
quality control department 品管部
research and development
department 研發部

職稱

高階管理者

chairman　董事長

president　總裁

vice president　副總裁

general manager　總經理

chief executive officer (CEO)　執行長

中階主管

manager　經理

assistant manager　副理

junior manager　襄理

section manager　課長

行政人員

clerk　事務員

assistant　助理

specialist　專員

representative　代表

工程師

engineer　工程師

technician　技師；技術人員

象限科技公司的總經理戴倫（Darren）拜訪艾普鐵克軟體公司。史蒂夫（Steve）和克莉絲汀（Christine）向他介紹公司概況……

S = Steve   D = Darren   C = Christine

S: I'd like to welcome you to AppTek Software. It's our pleasure to have Sector Technologies here today.

D: We're excited to be here.

S: Now, Christine Hicks will give a brief **overview**[1] of our company.

C: Thank you. AppTek Software was founded three years ago. Our original focus was on creating software for PCs. As market trends have shifted, though, we have **turned to** creating software for mobile devices. Yet, our mission has always remained the same. We want to make information more **accessible**[2] and understandable.

歡迎你們來到艾普鐵克軟體。很開心今天邀請象限科技來這裡。

我們很高興來這裡。

那麼，克莉絲汀·希克斯將簡短介紹我們公司。

謝謝。艾普鐵克創立於三年前。我們原先專注在個人電腦軟體的製造上。然而，當市場潮流改變時，我們轉而開發行動裝置的軟體。不過，我們的宗旨始終如一。我們想讓資訊更容易取得且更為人所了解。

Vocabulary

1. **overview** [ˋovəͺvju] *n.* 概要
   This chart gives us an overview of our performance over the last quarter.

2. **accessible** [ɛkˋsɛsəbəl] *adj.* 可取得的
   An order form is accessible through the business's website.

D: And have you been able to do this?

那麼你們有能力達成這個目標嗎？

C: We certainly believe so. Our front-end applications have been praised for their **ease of use**, and our back-end programs have always been stable and reliable. Today, we are focusing on developing software for the **booming**[3] mobile market. Already, we have seen our sales double over the last two quarters as a result.

我們當然這麼相信。我們的前端應用軟體因易於使用而備受讚譽，我們的後端程式則一直很穩定且可靠。今日，我們專注於開發蓬勃手機市場的軟體。就成果而言，我們前兩季的銷售額已成長兩倍。

S: This, **in turn**, has enabled us to expand our R & D department.

結果這讓我們得以擴編研發部。

C: Right. Research and development is **at the heart of** AppTek Software. We currently have a dedicated team of 25 in our R & D department. They **specialize**[4] in everything from mobile app development to customized software creation. It is their innovation that drives our company forward.

對的。研究與開發一直是艾普鐵克軟體的核心。我們目前在研發部擁有全心投入的 25 人團隊。他們專司行動應用程式開發到客製化軟體創造的所有領域。他們的創新力驅使公司邁步向前。

S: If you'd like to take a closer look at the creative side of AppTek, we can visit our R & D department next.

若你們想要細探艾普鐵克的創意面，接下來可視察我們的研發部。

D: Sounds great. I'd love to have a look.

聽起來不錯。我想參觀一下。

---

3. **booming** [ˈbumɪŋ] *adj.* 景氣好的
Booming tablet sales look set to continue this year.

4. **specialize** [ˈspɛʃəˌlaɪz] *v.* 專攻
The auto dealership specializes in luxury vehicles.

Part B 辦公室導覽

史蒂夫與克莉絲汀帶領戴倫一行人
參觀艾普鐵克軟體的運作情形……

S = Steve　　C = Christine　　D = Darren

S: Let's **pull back the curtain** on where the magic happens. This is our creative department.

讓我們揭曉魔法發生之處吧。這是我們的創意部。

C: Yes. Our creative department always **comes up with** new ideas that shake the entire industry.

是的。我們的創意部總是能想出震撼整個產業的新概念。

S: Indeed. Moving on, this is our R & D department. As you can see, it's quite large.

的確。往下走,這裡是我們的研發部。如你所見,這個部門規模滿大的。

Vocabulary

1. **mention** [ˈmɛnʃən] *v.* 提到
   Karla had mentioned she would be late today during the last meeting.

2. **devote** [dɪˈvot] *v.* 將……用於
   Mandy devotes her free time to teaching art to local children.

C: As I **mentioned**[1] earlier, we have a staff of 25 working on R & D. This team here, for example, specializes in voice-recognition software.

如我先前所提到的，我們有 25 名研發人員。例如這個小組專精的是語音辨識軟體。

D: How much of your budget is dedicated to R & D?

你們有多少預算是撥給研發的？

S: **Generally speaking**, we **devote**[2] 10 percent of our budget to our R & D efforts.

一般來說，我們投入預算的 10% 於研發工作中。

C: And this may even increase. That group over there is working on applications that will be **compatible**[3] with a variety of mobile devices.

這數字甚至可能會增加。那邊那個團隊正在開發能與多種行動裝置相容的應用程式。

D: Such as tablets, PDAs, and smartphones?

像是平板電腦、PDA 與智慧型手機嗎？

C: Exactly. And these new applications fit perfectly with the needs of Sector Technologies.

沒錯。而這些新的應用程式完美符合象限科技的需求。

D: You've definitely **got my attention**. Can we take a **sneak peek** at some of the apps that are being developed?

你真的吸引我的注意了。我們能先看看正在開發中的一些應用程式嗎？

C: Right this way. We'd love to get your input and **feedback**.[4]

往這兒走。我們很樂意得到你們的意見與回饋。

3. **compatible** [kəmˋpætəbəl]
   adj. 可相容的
   I downloaded a media player for my laptop, but it's not compatible with the operating system.

4. **feedback** [ˋfidˌbæk]
   n. 反應；回饋
   We welcome your feedback after you've had a chance to use our product.

重點筆記

1. *turn to* 轉而選擇……

說明	turn to 在英文中的常見用法有：

Ⓐ 轉而選擇……（對話用法）

- After I hurt my leg running, I turned to swimming to get exercise.
  跑步傷了腿之後，我轉而以游泳來做運動。

Ⓑ 向……尋求幫助或指教

- There are plenty of colleagues you can turn to for advice.
  有很多同事是你可以尋求建議的。

2. *ease of use* 簡易使用

說明	ease 為名詞，指「容易；不費力」，ease of use 即形容「使用上很便利」。

- This is a file transfer service with good performance and ease of use.
  這個文件傳輸服務的性能很好，且使用上很便利。

3. *in turn* 結果是……

說明	in turn 在英文中的常見用法有：

Ⓐ 結果是……（對話用法）

- When the quality of raw materials fell, the manufacturer, in turn, could not provide high-end products.
  當原物料品質下滑，結果就是製造商無法提供高檔的產品。

Ⓑ 依次；依序

- Each employee at the award ceremony stepped up to collect a prize in turn.
  頒獎典禮上的每個員工依次上台領獎。

4. *at the heart of* 在……的中心地帶

說明	此片語指「位於……的中心地帶」，暗示某事物具有相對的重要性。

- At the heart of the matter is the company's inability to compete with larger rivals.

  這件事的重點是該公司沒有能力與大型對手競爭。

5. *pull back the curtain* 一窺究竟；好戲登場

說明	curtain 可指「窗簾；門簾」或「舞台布幕」，此用語的字面義是「把簾幕拉到後面；拉起簾幕」，引申為「一窺究竟」或「好戲登場」的意思。另外，behind the curtain 照字面解釋為「在布幕的後面」，可用來比喻「在幕後；私底下」。

- The developer decided to pull back the curtain and reveal how he had thought of the technique.

  研發者決定揭曉他是如何想出該項技術。

- If you had been involved in the project, you would have known what happened behind the curtain.

  如果你參與了這個專案，你就會知道背後發生了什麼事。

6. *come up with* 想出；提出

說明	此用法形容經過思考和發展而得到某種結果，常用來表示「想出方法；找出解答」。另外，口語中的 come up with 還有「湊出；拿出（錢）」的意思。

- Randal came up with a way to cut our budget without laying off employees.

  藍道想出辦法來縮減我們的預算而不必裁員。

- Claire came up with enough money to afford a trip abroad this holiday season.

  克萊兒湊出足夠的錢在這次的假期季節出國旅行。

7. *generally speaking* 一般而言

說明	generally speaking 為獨立分詞片語，通常置於句首做強調，並用逗點與主要子句隔開，意同 generally 和 in general。

- Generally speaking, Peter likes exercising in the morning rather than the evening.
  一般而言，彼得喜歡在早上運動勝過在下午運動。
- In general, if you eat too much and don't get enough exercise, you will gain weight.
  一般來說，如果你吃太多又沒有足夠的運動，體重就會增加。

8. *get sb's attention* 引起某人的注意

說明	attention 指「專心；注意」，常見搭配用法如下：

A attract/draw/get sb's attention 引起某人的注意（對話用法）

- The sign in the store window got the woman's attention.
  商店櫥窗上的招牌吸引了這名女子的注意。

B give/pay one's attention to N./V-ing （某人）專心於……

- The teacher gave her full attention to the student who was reading aloud.
  老師全神貫注地聽那個大聲朗讀的學生。

9. *sneak peek* 搶先看；預告

說明	sneek 指「偷偷摸摸行動」，peek 指「偷看」，sneak peek 則形容「優先預覽（某物正式提供之前的觀看機會）」，亦可作 sneak preview。

- The company is offering a sneak peek at its new software.
  該公司正提供其新軟體的預覽試用。
- The director screened a sneak peek of his latest film.
  這個導演放映了他最新電影的一段預告片。

延伸學習

完美公司簡介三步驟

100%

Step 1

What We Do 背景介紹
歡迎潛在顧客。就公司的背景、發展與目標做簡短報告。

Welcome to Computer Tech, gentlemen. The head office here was established in 1995, and it's where we house our design teams.

歡迎各位來到電腦科技。這裡的總公司建立於 1995 年，我們的設計團隊也位於此處。

Step 2

More Detail 提供細節
說明更深入的細節，描述產品與服務，並舉出一些事實或數據。

Our business is really thriving. The number of purchase orders we receive each month has gone up by nearly 30 percent since the beginning of the year.

我們的業務蒸蒸日上。自今年年初起，我們每月收到的訂單數量已增加將近三成。

Step 3

Parts of the Whole 公司部門介紹
介紹特定部門時，說明他們的職責以及他們對公司與客戶所做出的貢獻。

Here is the R & D department. This is the group of people in charge of designing the products we sell and making sure that they all meet our clients' specifications. Without the dedication of the talented men and women in this department, there's no way that our organization would be such an industry leader.

這裡是研發部門。本團隊負責設計我們所販賣的商品，並確保都能達到客戶的規格需求。若沒有本部門優秀成員們的貢獻，我們公司不可能成為業界的領導者。

圖解簡報現場 🎧 PLAY ALL

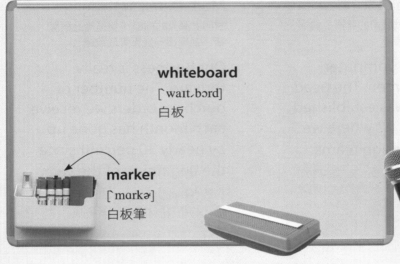

whiteboard
[ˈwaɪtˌbɔrd]
白板

marker
[ˈmɑrkə]
白板筆

whiteboard eraser
[ɪˈresə]
白板擦

wired microphone
[waɪrd] [ˈmaɪkrəˌfon]
有線麥克風

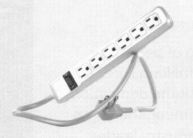

power strip
[strɪp]
延長線

laptop
[ˈlæpˌtɑp]
筆記型電腦

52

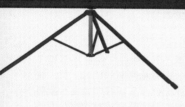

projection screen
[prə`dʒɛkʃən] [skrin]
投影布幕

laser pointer
[`lezə] [`pɔɪntə]
雷射光筆

cordless/portable microphone
[`kɔrdləs] [`pɔrtəbəl]
無線麥克風

clip-on microphone
[`klɪp͵ɑn]
領夾式麥克風（小蜜蜂）

adapter
[ə`dæptə]
轉接頭

digital projector
[`dɪdʒətl̩] [prə`dʒɛktə]
數位投影機

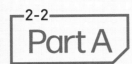

公司背景介紹

約翰（John）向來訪的外賓介紹自己的公司。

J = John

J: Good afternoon, gentlemen. I'm John Lin from the sales team at KYO Electronics. Thank you for meeting with us today. I'll be giving you a **brief**[1] overview of who we are and what we can offer.

男士們，午安。我是 KYO 電子公司業務團隊的約翰‧林。感謝你們今天與我們會面。我將向你們簡略介紹敝司以及我們所能提供的服務。

We are a precision prototyping, tooling, and manufacturing company and have been **operating**[2] for over 30 years. We **specialize in** CAD, CAM, advanced 3D printing, and precision CNC machining.

我們是家精密模型製作、開模與製造公司，營運時間已超過三十年。我們專精於電腦輔助設計、電腦輔助製造、先進 3D 列印以及精密電腦數值控制加工。

Vocabulary

1. **brief** [brif] *adj.* 簡短的
   Keep your business pitch brief, or you risk losing audience members with short attention spans.

2. **operate** [ˋɑpəˏret] *v.* 營運；運作
   Our company has been operating in Southeast Asia since we went international in the early 2000s.

3. **substantial** [səbˋstænʃəl] *adj.* 大量的；重大的
   Netflix's willingness to take risks has allowed it to maintain a substantial lead over its competition.

KYO Electronics offers **substantial**[3] advantages over our competitors. Our 24-hour service and support is **unmatched**[4] in the industry. Our flexible design capabilities and optimized facilities allow us to provide extremely cost-effective solutions. Additionally,* we have global reach* and are **well versed**[5] in international regulation compliance.

Our mid-term goal is to expand our global presence by adding locations in key markets. Long-term, our goal is to establish a rapid prototyping center in Silicon Valley.

Thank you for your time. Do you have any questions?

KYO 電子公司提供的大量優勢凌駕於我們的競爭對手。我們的全天候服務和支援在業界無與倫比。我們彈性的設計能力和優化的設備,讓我們能提供極具成本效益的解決方案。此外,敝司的服務範圍遍及全球,我們亦精通國際合規。

我們的中期目標是在主要市場新增駐點以拓展全球能見度。展望長期,我們的目標是在矽谷建立快速模型中心。

謝謝兩位寶貴的時間。你們有任何問題嗎?

4. **unmatched** [ˌʌnˋmætʃt] *adj.* 無與倫比的
Although many companies copy Apple, the build quality of its devices has been unmatched for over a decade.

5. **well versed** [ˌwɛlˋvɝst]
adj. 精通的(+ in)
Daniel's answers to the interviewers' questions showed that he is well versed in current social media trends.

字彙補給站

* **additionally** [əˋdɪʃənəli]
adv. 另外地

* **reach** [ritʃ] *n.* 可及範圍

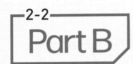

Part B 介紹產品及服務

約翰與外賓柯林（Colin）和托姆（Thom）進行公司簡介後的會談。

C = Colin　　T = Thom　　J = John

C: So, John, your facilities have certainly **piqued our interest**.

約翰，你們的設備確實引起我們的興趣。

T: Yes, especially your industrial-standard five-axis* CNC machine.

是啊，尤其是你們工業標準的五軸電腦數控機器。

J: Our precision prototype tooling equipment can **ensure**[1] a rapid turnaround* for your end product.* We're quite proud of it.

我們的精密原型模具設備可確保你們的最終產品能有快速的製成時間。我們對此相當自豪。

Vocabulary

1. **ensure** [ɪnˋʃʊr] v. 確保
   Each department has standards in place to ensure that work can continue despite incidents or emergencies.

2. **humble** [ˋhʌmbəl] adj. 不起眼的；謙遜的
   TimeCorp's CEO was well known for being quite humble about his company's success.

3. **boast** [bost] v. 以擁有……而自豪
   In addition to her skills at graphic design, Rachel boasts web development and programming abilities.

4. **employ** [ɪmˋplɔɪ] v. 雇用；利用
   Cambridge Analytica is accused of employing questionable methods in order to obtain user data.

C: With good reason. Please continue.

合情合理。請繼續。

J: From our **humble**[2] beginnings in 1987 as an OEM, KYO has **grown into** a multinational manufacturer that **boasts**[3] state-of-the-art machining and support services for designers.

自 1987 年的不起眼代工廠開始，KYO 公司壯大成以提供設計師最先進的加工和支援服務而自豪的跨國製造商。

T: That is some truly impressive growth.

真是令人讚嘆的成長。

J: We **employ**[4] a dedicated* team of over 1,000 staff spread across seven departments and two countries, all <u>committed to</u> our clients' needs.

我們聘用一千多名員工所組成的專職團隊，橫跨七個部門及兩個國家，全都盡心盡力滿足客戶的需求。

commit to sth 指「承諾、表態、保證某事物」。

C: It sounds like you've **assembled**[5] quite a team.

聽起來你們組成了挺不錯的團隊。

aim 當動詞表示「旨在⋯⋯；致力於⋯⋯；以⋯⋯為目標」，應用句型有 aim to + V. 和 aim at/for + N./V-ing。

J: Now, we're <u>aiming to</u> make an impact stateside* with the goal of becoming the **go-to**[6] rapid prototyping center for all of Silicon Valley. That's where you **come in**.

我們打算在美國境內發揮影響力，目標是成為全矽谷快速模型中心的第一把交椅。這也是你們可以協助的地方。

---

5. **assemble** [əˋsɛmbəl] *v.* 聚集；召集
   If we're going to film a new TV spot, we'll need to assemble a crew.

6. **go-to** [ˏgoˋtu]
   adj. （為解決某問題）必找的（人事物）
   Aaron is the go-to person in HR for questions about current labor laws.

字彙補給站

* **axis** [ˋæksəs] *n.* 軸
* **turnaround** [ˋtɜnəˏraʊnd] *n.* 製成時間
* **end product** *n.* 最終產品；製成品
* **dedicated** [ˋdɛdəˏketəd] *adj.* 盡心盡力的
* **stateside** [ˋstetˏsaɪd] *adv.* 美國地

重點筆記

1. *specialize in*　專精於……

說明	specialize [ˋspɛʃəˌlaɪz] 指對一門學科、研究或技術知之甚詳，或花了很多時間和精力去研究、學習，in 後面加上所專精的事物或領域。

- Accountants that specialize in cryptocurrency and its tax implications are becoming more and more commonplace.
  專精於加密貨幣及其稅務解釋的會計師越來越普遍了。

2. *pique sb's interest*　引起某人的興趣

說明	pique [pik] 指「激起；刺激」，pique sb's interest 即形容「引起某人的興趣」。

- Power Tea's unusual advertisements piqued Chris's interest and caused him to buy the drink.
  強力茶不尋常的廣告引起克里斯的興趣，讓他去買了這款飲料。

3. *with good reason*　合情合理

說明	此片語用來形容某事物因為已經過證明而有充分正當的理由或目的。

- American elections often cause markets to rise or fall — and with good reason.
  美國大選常會導致市場的漲跌——合情合理。

4. *grow into*　逐漸發展成……

說明	此片語原指「逐漸長大成……」，引申有「逐漸發展成……」之意。

- It was originally just a small outdoor concert, but it has grown into one of the largest music festivals in the world.
  它原本只是小型的戶外音樂會，但已逐漸發展成世界上最大的音樂節之一。

5. *quite a(n) sth* 很是……；相當……的

說明	quite 做副詞，指「相當」，注意在此用法中，a(n) 要放在 quite 之後。quite a(n) sth「某事物很、相當……」可用來強調某事物的程度或數量。

- My friend Mark is quite a joker, so you never know what he's going to do.
  我朋友馬克是個很愛開玩笑的人，所以你永遠不知道他接下來會做什麼。

6. *come in* 參與

說明	come in 在英文中的常見用法有：

Ⓐ 參與；派上用場（對話用法）

- Ron needs a positive role model, and that's where his uncle Phil comes in.
  榮恩需要正面的模範，而這正是他的叔叔菲爾能扮演的角色。

Ⓑ 表比賽名次

- Rob came in last in the race because he hurt his knee.
  羅伯在賽跑中得到最後一名，因為他膝蓋受傷了。

Ⓒ 以……的樣式、種類販售

- This car model comes in three different colors that you can choose from.
  這個車款有三種不同的顏色供你選擇。

Ⓓ 上市

- The latest models of the popular game system will come in next week.
  這個當紅遊戲系列的最新版本下星期會上市。

延伸學習

技術小詞典

computer-aided design (CAD)
電腦輔助設計
使用電腦軟體製作並模擬實物設計，以展現新開發商品的外型、結構、色彩、質感等特色的過程。

original equipment manufacturer (OEM)
原始設備製造商
受採購方所託，負責提供設備、技術和人力以生產商品的製造商，俗稱「代工廠商」或「委託製造商」。

computer-aided manufacturing (CAM)
電腦輔助製造
使用電腦進行生產設備的管理、控制和操作的過程。

computer numerical control (CNC)
電腦數值控制
透過事先設定的指令進行自動加工，並由電腦負責整合控制，目前的數值控制工具機大多利用電腦來運算處理。

公司簡介必用句型

From our beginnings in (year), (company name) has grown into a multinational company that boasts . . .
自（年分）開始，（公司名）壯大成以……而自豪的跨國公司。

We are a (type) company and have been operating for (number) years.
我們是（類型）公司，營運時間已有（數目）年。

We employ a dedicated team of (number) staff spread across . . .
我們聘用（數量）名員工所組成的專職團隊，橫跨……

We have worked hard since our establishment to build a reputation for . . .
自成立以來，我們一直努力建立……的聲譽。

Our short-term/mid-term/long-term goal is to . . .
我們的短／中／長期目標是……

Our (product/service) allows us to provide . . .
我們的（產品／服務）讓我們能提供……

We're aiming to . . . with the goal of becoming . . .
我們打算……，目標是成為……

2-3 Explaining the Management Structure
介紹公司組織 I

公司導覽必備句型 🔊 PLAY ALL

句型 1

（某部門）領導／負責（某工作項目）		
The (department) +	lead guide direct conduct	+ (work/task/ assignment).

- The director asked that the HR department lead a training session for new employees.
  總監要求人資部負責新進員工的訓練課程。

- The engineering department is conducting tests on our software.
  工程部正在測試我們的軟體。

句型 2

（某工作項目）由（某部門）負責		
It +	(be) the duty (be) the obligation (be) the responsibility	+ of (department) + to (do work/task/assignment).

- It is the responsibility of the accounting department to do the annual audit.
  年度稽查由會計部負責。

- It is the duty of each department to update the spreadsheets before the end of the month.
  在月底之前更新試算表是每個部門的職責。

句型 3

（某人）領導／負責（某部門／專案）		
(Name) +	run head manage (be) in charge of (be) responsible for (be) accountable for	+ the (department/ project).

- Kenny Winters heads the public relations department.
  肯尼‧溫特斯領導公關部。

- Sara and Martin manage the team of customer service representatives.
  莎拉和馬丁負責管理客服代表團隊。

- George Baker is in charge of the Elite project.
  喬治‧貝克負責伊利特專案。

句型 4

（某部門／專案）由（某人）主導／負責		
The (department/ project) +	fall under (be) under the direction of (be) under the leadership of (be) under the jurisdiction of (be) under the responsibility of	+ (name).

- The financial department falls under Holly Milton.
  財務部由荷莉‧米爾頓主導。

- The sales team is under the direction of Mr. Norton.
  業務團隊是由諾頓先生所帶領的。

Part A　介紹公司組織

蒂娜（Tina）向廠商派駐的合作夥伴大衛（David）介紹公司的領導階層及部門的運作情形……

T = Tina　　D = David

T： Hi, David. I'm Tina, and I'll be showing you around. I'd like to start by explaining the structure of our corporation. The chairman and CEO of JRC Electronics is a gentleman by the name of Philip Morton. Mr. Morton has more than 25 years of experience in the industry.

D： Is it true he worked as a software developer before he got into electronics?

嗨，大衛。我是蒂娜，我會帶你到處看看。我想先說明我們公司的組織架構。JRC 電子公司的董事長暨執行長是個名為菲力普‧摩頓的男士。摩頓先生在業界已有超過 25 年的經驗。

他在進入電子業之前曾是個軟體開發師，是真的嗎？

Vocabulary

1. **cofounder** [ˌkoˋfaʊndə] *n.* 共同創辦人
   He is the cofounder of this company.

2. **oversee** [ˌovəˋsi] *v.* 監督；管理
   As supervisor, it is my job to oversee the construction of the building.

3. **day-to-day** [ˋdetəˋde] *adj.* 日常的
   Susie likes her job because her day-to-day responsibilities vary.

T: Yes, it is. He worked for Minisoft **way back in the day**. After leaving that company, he became one of the **cofounders**[1] of JRC, so he really understands this business at the core level.

是的，沒錯。他過去在 Minisoft 公司工作。離開那家公司之後，他成為 JRC 公司的共同創辦人，所以他對這個產業有核心程度的了解。

Our president and COO is Larry Garcia. He has been with the company for 10 years and has been in the management side for about eight.

我們的總裁暨營運長是賴瑞‧賈西亞。他在公司十年了，在管理階層則大約八年的時間。

D: What does he handle?

他負責什麼呢？

T: He **oversees**[2] the **day-to-day**[3] operations, including issues in the Legal, Public Relations, and Occupational Health & Safety Offices.

他監督日常運作，包括法務、公關以及職業健康與安全辦公室相關的問題。

D: And the HR manager is?

那人資經理……？

T: Responsible for all our human resource needs is that man right there, Fred Darabont. He is the man to talk to whenever you have **administrative**[4]-type problems.

負責我們所有人資需求的是那邊那位先生，弗雷德‧達拉邦特。你有行政類別的問題時，可找他談。

D: That's good to know. Thanks for the **rundown**,[5] Tina. I look forward to finding out more about how things work here.

很高興知道這點。謝謝你的簡介，蒂娜。我期待更進一步了解這裡的運作方式。

---

4. **administrative** [əd`mɪnəstrətɪv]
   adj. 行政的；管理的
   He works in an administrative position.

5. **rundown** [`rʌn͵daʊn]
   n. 扼要報告；概要說明
   Please give me a rundown on yesterday's activities.

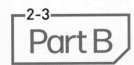

Part B　介紹重要幹部

蒂娜接著向大衛說明跟他會有業務往來的主要幹部，以及相關部門的基本運作方式……

T = Tina　　D = David

T：Now that we've talked about the big bosses at the company, I'd like to take you around and show you the people you'll **deal with**[1] more directly.

既然我們已談過公司的重要人物，我想帶你到處看看並介紹你會有直接業務往來的人。

Our **division**[2] director is Jack McFarland. He's in charge of the six departments in our division. The first one here is Procurement, and the manager is Doris Gill.

我們的事業處總監是傑克·麥法蘭德。他掌管我們事業處的六個部門。第一個就是採購部，經理是朵莉絲·吉爾。

D：OK. And who heads up Quality Control?

好的。那誰帶領品管部？

T：That would be Frank Moore. He's been with the company since the start.

是法蘭克·摩爾。他從一開始就在公司工作了。

Vocabulary

1. **deal with** v. 應對；處理
   Brian dealt with the problem before going home for the day.

2. **division** [dəˋvɪʒən] n. 事業處
   Mr. Bennett is in charge of that division.

3. **run** [rʌn] v. 管理
   Mindy used to run this department, but she quit yesterday.

D： Can you tell me more about the marketing and sales departments?

T： Sure. Kate Townsend leads a team of six in Marketing. She's been with us for seven years.

Our sales department is **run**[3] by Steven Hill. He has four employees reporting directly to him at the moment. They've been meeting weekly because they're under a **tight**[4] deadline and currently **short-staffed**.[5]

D： Hmm. And what about the VP of operations? Who reports to him?

T： There are two managers from our division who report to him as well as the division director. They are our marketing manager and our business operations manager, Joseph Jackson.

D： Well, that seems like a lot to remember. I hope I can **keep everyone straight**.

T： Don't worry. You'll be fine. Now follow me, and I'll show you to your office.

能告訴我更多關於行銷及業務部的事嗎？

當然。凱特‧唐森德帶領行銷部的六人團隊。她在公司七年了。

我們的業務部是由史蒂芬‧希爾所管理的。目前有四名員工是他的直屬下屬。因為他們面臨緊迫的截止期限，且目前人手不足，所以他們每週都會固定開會。

嗯。那營運副總呢？誰對他直接負責？

我們的事業處有兩位經理要向他和總監報告工作狀況。他們是行銷經理以及事業營運部經理喬瑟夫‧傑克森。

嗯，似乎有太多要記的了。希望我可以把每個人都記清楚。

別擔心。你沒問題的。現在跟著我，我帶你去你的辦公室。

---

4. **tight** [taɪt] *adj.* 緊迫的；吃緊的
The company is on a tight budget while the economy is in decline.

5. **short-staffed** [ˌʃɔrtˋstæft] *adj.* 人手短缺的
We are struggling right now because the place is short-staffed.

重點筆記

1. *way back in the day* 很久以前

說明	back in the day 指「過去」，而非特定的某一天。way 在此為副詞，表示「很；非常」，有加強語氣的作用，way back in the day 即強調「非常久以前的過去」。

- Way back in the day, my dad played drums in a rock band!
  很久以前，我爸爸曾擔任搖滾樂團的鼓手！

2. *head up* 主導；領導

說明	head 當動詞有「領導；主管」的意思，片語 head up 即指「負責（團隊）；帶領（部門）」。

- Val heads up the entertainment committee in this office.
  維爾主導公司裡的康樂委員會。

3. *keep sb/sth straight* 弄清楚某人事物

說明	straight 做形容詞除了指「筆直的」，亦可表示「有條理的」。keep sb/sth straight 即形容「弄清楚某人事物」，特別是不被混淆地清楚分辨性質相似的人事物。另外，straight 亦常做副詞，表「連續地」。

- These two bottles look so much alike. It's hard to keep them straight.
  這兩個瓶子看起來好像，很難分得清楚。
- The contestants danced for 10 hours straight.
  參賽者連續跳舞跳了十個小時。

延伸學習

看懂公司組織圖

請看以下組織圖範例，並回答下方的三個問題。

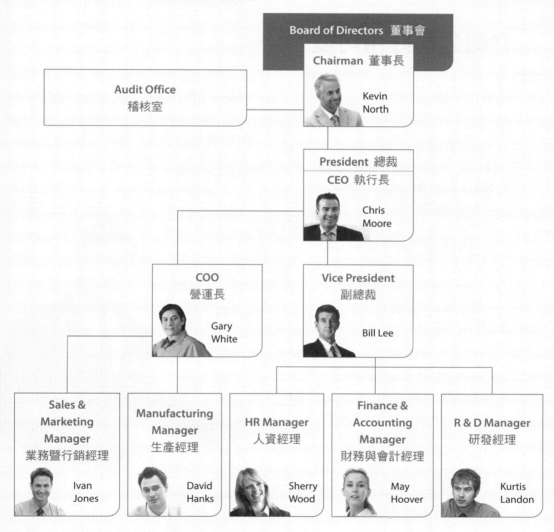

❶ Which two positions does Chris Moore hold?

❷ Who reports to the Chief Operating Officer?

❸ Who does the R & D Manager directly report to?

介紹公司好用句型 🔊 PLAY ALL

公司沿革

Time Trial Inc. was founded in 2012 and is now the world's fastest-growing shoelace manufacturer.

時淬公司創立於 2012 年,現在是全世界成長最快速的鞋帶製造商。

Hera Pharmaceuticals was founded in 1952 and is now a leader in cancer research.

赫拉藥廠創立於 1952 年,現在是癌症研究的領導者。

營運策略

Our original focus was on manufacturing quality formal wear, but since the 1980s, we have shifted strategies to reach younger customers.

我們原本專注於量產高品質的禮服,但從 1980 年代開始,我們轉換策略以觸及更年輕的客群。

Our original focus was on building skyscrapers, but since 2009, we have shifted strategies to become New York's leading property management firm.

我們原本專注於建造摩天大樓,但從 2009 年開始,我們轉換策略,成為紐約主要的物業管理公司。

發展願景

Our mission is to **provide customers with intuitive solutions** for optimizing work flow.

我們的使命是提供顧客可優化工作流程的直覺解決方案。

Our vision is to **improve people's quality of life** through our products.

我們的願景是透過我們的產品來改善人們的生活品質。

人員職掌

Jennifer Tully **runs** trials of all new medicines developed by our company.

珍妮佛‧塔利負責測試公司開發的所有新藥物。

Lin Rhodes is **in charge of** recruiting and hiring recent college graduates.

琳‧羅德斯負責招聘應屆大學畢業生。

部門從屬

The human resources department is **under the direction of** Hal Donahue.

人資部門由哈爾‧唐納修所帶領。

Accounts Receivable **falls under the responsibility of** Olivia Pearl.

應收帳款部門屬於奧利維亞‧波爾的責任範圍。

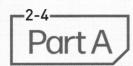 Part A 介紹公司沿革

歐羅拉廣告公司的業務經理潔西卡（Jessica）和創意部副理維克特（Victor）向來訪的滋補營養品公司企畫總監納森（Nathan）及企畫專員蘿倫（Lauren）介紹公司的概況。

J = Jessica　　N = Nathan　　V = Victor　　L = Lauren

J： Welcome to Aurora Advertising. Please allow me to introduce Victor. He'll be **running the show** today.

N： Pleasure meeting you. I'm **keen**[1] to hear what you have to say.

歡迎來到歐羅拉廣告公司。請容我介紹維克特，今天的簡報由他主導。

很高興認識你。我非常期待你所要介紹的內容。

Vocabulary

1. **keen** [kin] *adj.* 熱切的；渴望的
   The board members are keen on finding effective ways to reduce costs.

2. **cutting-edge** [ˏkʌtɪŋ ˋɛdʒ] *adj.* 最新潮的；最尖端的
   Google employs cutting-edge technology on its fleet of Google Street View cars.

3. **shift** [ʃɪft] *v.* 轉換
   Management is shifting focus away from the less profitable divisions.

4. **holistic** [hoˋlɪstɪk] *adj.* 全面的
   In order to maximize profits, we've taken a holistic view of possible investment opportunities.

V： Great. **Let's get to it** then. As you know, Aurora was founded in 1978 and is now the ninth-largest advertiser in the world. Our original focus was on creating **cutting-edge**[2] content for traditional media, but since 2005, we've **shifted**[3] strategies to develop a more **holistic**[4] approach.

太好了。我們開始吧。如你們所知，歐羅拉公司創立於 1978 年，現在是全世界第九大的廣告商。我們原本專注於創造適合傳統媒體的新潮內容，但從 2005 年開始，我們轉換策略，開發更全面的途徑。

L： Does that mean you're focusing more now on digital?

那意味著你們現在更專注在數位方面嗎？

V： Not necessarily. The proprietary* multichannel advertising platform we've developed allows us to **zero in on** specific demographics* on a variety of mediums* — not just online.

不盡然如此。我們開發的專利多管道廣告平台讓我們可在各種媒介上鎖定特定客群——不只是在網路上而已。

L： Then it's innovation that **sets you apart**?

那麼是創新使你們與眾不同的嗎？

J： Innovation and authenticity.* Our mission is to **ensure** customers develop a **genuine**[5] connection to your products no matter where they **come across** your ads.

創新和可靠性。我們的使命是確保消費者無論在哪裡看到廣告，都能與你們的產品發展出真正的連結。

N： Now that's an <u>out-of-the-box</u> approach we can **get behind**.

那是個我們能支持的別出心裁方法。

指「非傳統的、非制式的」。
源自片語 think out/outside of the box「跳脫框架思考」。

5. **genuine** [ˋdʒɛnjəwən]
adj. 真正的；真誠的
Harley-Davidson fans have a genuine love for the company and their motorbikes.

字彙補給站

✳ **proprietary** [prəˋpraɪəˏtɛri] *adj.* 專利的

✳ **demographic** [ˏdɛməˋgræfɪk]
n. （顧客）族群

✳ **medium** [ˋmidiəm] *n.* 媒介

✳ **authenticity** [ˏɔθɛnˋtɪsəti] *n.* 可靠性

Part B 介紹企業架構

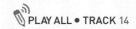

維克特繼續介紹公司的組織架構和各領導階層的職掌。

V = Victor   L = Lauren   N = Nathan   J = Jessica

V: You may have heard there's been a recent **shake-up**[1] at the company. Our founder Frank Lloyds **stepped down** as CEO and **tapped**[2] Wayland Müller to **head**[3] the company.

你們可能已聽說我們公司最近進行改組。我們的創辦人法蘭克·羅伊德斯卸下執行長一職，並欽點偉蘭·穆勒帶領公司。

L: We were **aware**.[4] What about you, Victor? Where do you **fit into** all of this?

我們知道。你呢，維克特？你在這之中歸屬何處？

Vocabulary

1. **shake-up** [ˈʃek͵ʌp] *n.* 重新改組
   The president of the company announced there would be a shake-up in management.

2. **tap** [tæp] *v.* 欽點；指定
   Lidia was tapped by Arthur to redesign our company's outlet stores.

3. **head** [hɛd] *v.* 領導；帶領
   While Angel is out on vacation, Terrence is heading the accounting department.

以字面義「第二指揮」引申指「副手」。

V： I'm Lessidi Pretorius' second-in-command in Creative. We're **overseen**[5] by the COO, Mark Hull, as are Jessica and our marketing manager Denis Tucker.

我在創意部門，是勒西迪‧普利托里爾斯的副手。我們都由營運長馬克‧霍爾監管，潔西卡和我們的行銷經理丹尼斯‧塔克也是。

N： We know you're the sales manager, Jessica, but what exactly does that position **entail**?[6]

潔西卡，我們知道你是業務經理，但那個職位的確切職掌為何？

J： I mostly manage relationships with marquee clients such as yourselves, Tonka-Cola, and Carville.

我大多管理與貴司、唐卡可樂及卡維爾公司等重要客戶的關係。

marquee [mɑr`ki] 指「（入口處的）遮篷」，marquee client 即以字面義「大門口的客戶」引申指「重要客戶」。

L： What about the other departments?

那其他部門呢？

V： Research and Online Development, Human Resources, and Finance and Accounting all fall under the direction of Vice President Vanessa Murk as well as the managers of each department — Nicholas Long in R & D, Aiko Ito in HR, and Joan West in Accounting.

網路研發部、人資部和財會部皆由副董事長凡妮莎‧穆克管轄，研發的尼可拉斯‧隆恩、人資的伊藤愛子和會計的瓊恩‧衛斯特等各部門經理也歸她管。

N： Great. I think that about **sorts out** all our questions.

非常好，我想我們全部的問題都差不多釐清了。

---

4. **aware** [ə`wɛr] *adj.* 知曉
   I wasn't aware Jennifer would be out of the office the whole month.

5. **oversee** [ˌovə`si] *v.* 監管
   Jordan and Edith oversee the planning committee and are responsible for the Christmas party.

6. **entail** [ɛn`tel] *v.* 使必要；牽涉
   Getting the project in on time entails some overtime and a lot of hard work.

重點筆記

1. *run the show* 主導

說明	字面義為「進行表演」，用來比喻「主掌；操縱」，相當於 be in charge、be in command。

- Warren Buffet has run the show at Berkshire Hathaway since 1962.
  華倫‧巴菲特自 1962 年起主導波克夏‧海瑟威控股公司。

2. *Let's get to it.* 我們開始吧。

說明	get to 指「抵達、達到」，全句以字面義「讓我們去到那兒吧。」示意和引導大家「進入正題」。

A: We need to finish this report by tomorrow.
　我們得在明天以前完成這份報告。

B: Let's get to it.
　我們開始吧。

3. *approach* 途徑；方法

說明	approach [ə`protʃ] 當名詞的常見意思如下：

Ⓐ 途徑；方法（對話用法）

- Keith's approach to the project at work was very creative, so we let him lead the team.
  基斯對工作專案的方法很有創意，所以我們讓他領導小組。

Ⓑ 靠近；臨近

- Many kinds of birds fly south at the approach of winter.
  許多鳥兒在冬天來臨之際飛向南方。

4. *zero in on* 鎖定……；瞄準……

說明	此語原形容調整槍砲、標靶等的射擊位置，常用來比喻「瞄準目標；集中火力」，亦可引申指「把注意力全集中在某事物上」。

- The engineers managed to zero in on a solution to the design flaw.
  工程師成功找到設計缺陷的解決方案了。

5. *set sb apart* 使某人與眾不同

說明	此用法形容「使某人不同於其他人；使突出、顯眼」，後面可用 from 加上其他的人或物。另外，set apart 也可表示為了某特殊目的或用途「特別撥出、騰出」，同 set aside。

- What sets Jack apart from other employees is his passion for learning new things.
  使傑克特出於其他員工的是他對學習新事物的熱忱。

- Donna set apart some apples to make a pie later in the week.
  唐娜留了一些蘋果好在這週晚些時候可做派。

6. *ensure* 保證

說明	ensure [ɪnˋʃʊr] 指「確保、保證（某事物的發生）」，另一相似拼法的 assure [əˋʃʊr] 則指「（為消除憂慮而）向……保證」。

- Investing in training is necessary to ensure the continued success of a company.
  投資教育訓練以確保公司的持續成功是必要的。

- During the meeting, the CEO assured investors that sales would recover in Q3.
  會中，執行長向投資人保證業績會在第三季恢復。

7. *come across* 看到；無意中發現

說明	come across 在英文中的常見用法有：

Ⓐ 看到；無意中發現（對話用法）

- When we were moving offices, we came across some old photos of the company's founders.
  搬遷辦公室時，我們無意中發現了一些公司創立者的舊照片。

Ⓑ 給人（某種）印象

- John came across as quiet in the meeting, but he is really a loud, fun guy.
  約翰在會議中給人文靜的印象，但他實際上是個喧鬧風趣的人。

Ⓒ 還清（債務）

- Colby finally came across with the money he owed me.
  寇比終於還清他欠我的錢。

8. *get behind* 支持

說明	此片語的字面意思是「到⋯⋯後面」，用來喻指「支持」某人或某事。另外也可指「落後；拖延」，意思類似 fall behind。

- Everyone on the team got behind Haley's idea for the new product line.
  團隊的每個成員都支持海莉對於新系列產品的點子。

- I got very behind in my work because of the days I was out sick.
  因為我生病請假好幾天，我的工作進度落後很多。

9. *step down* 退職

說明	以「走下（台階）」的意象引申指「卸下（某職位）；辭職」，亦有「退休」的含意。類似用法有 bow out「鞠躬下台；辭職」。

- Denis stepped down from his position to spend more time with his family.
  丹尼斯卸下職位，好花更多時間來陪家人。

- Many investment bankers bow out of the profession early due to the pressure.
  許多投資銀行家因為壓力，很早就從此崗位中離開了。

10. *fit into* 安置

說明	此片語原指「安置；適合（某處）」，於對話中則表示某人在組織架構中所扮演的角色、位置。

- With her qualifications, Sara should fit into the job perfectly.
  以她的資歷，莎拉應該完全能勝任這份工作。

11. *sort out* 釐清；解決

說明	本片語原指「將……撿出、分類整理」，引申為「把……安排妥當、弄清楚」的意思。

- Fortunately, our supplier sorted out the issue with the delayed order immediately.
  幸運地，我們的供應商立即解決了訂單延誤的問題。

UNIT
3

Presenting to Win Clients
爭取客戶

3-1 Proposing a Strategic Alliance
合作提案 I

洽談合作實用句 🎧 PLAY ALL

界定目標市場

- **Our target demographic is millennial women.**
  我們的目標客群為千禧世代的女性。

- **We are aiming for customers in the 19- to 25-age range.**
  我們鎖定十九至二十五歲年齡範圍的顧客。

提議合作模式

- **I propose we manage distribution** while you **handle production.**
  我提議我們管理經銷，而你們處理生產的部分。

- **Our services complement each other so well that we should work together.**
  我們的服務完美互補，因此我們應該合作。

提出有力合作點

- **The group we're targeting has a history of rapidly adopting new technology.**
  我們的目標族群向來很快就能適應新的科技。

- **We've done our research on potential consumers, and we're convinced that we'd succeed in the market.**
  我們已對潛在消費者做過研究,並相信我們會在市場上取得成功。

討論成本和利潤

- **I believe the costs should be split fifty-fifty between the two companies.**
  我想成本應兩家公司平均分攤。

- **We'll have a 30 percent share of the profits on the sale of our co-branded products.**
  我們在聯名商品的銷售上將取得三成的利潤。

Part A 討論結盟合作

飯店行銷經理凱莉（Kelly）向餐廳行銷經理艾力克斯（Alex）、百貨行銷總監莎拉（Sarah）以及戲院行銷經理赫克特（Hector）提出合作計畫，四人討論可能的運作模式。

K = Kelly　　A = Alex　　S = Sarah　　H = Hector

K: The reason I've called you all here today is to **put forward** a plan to **unite**[1] our loyalty programs.

A: You've piqued my interest. How would it work?

K: I'm proposing that we build an ecosystem* of sorts with a card and app. We'd call it Dash Rewards, and it would help us **capitalize on** the overlap* between our different business sectors.*

我今天召集大家來這裡的原因是要提出一個聯合我們酬賓方案的計畫。

你引起我的興趣了。會如何進行呢？

我提議我們透過酬賓卡和應用程式來打造一個類生態圈。我們可稱之為飆風紅利計畫，它能讓我們從彼此不同產業間的交疊處獲利。

Vocabulary

1. **unite** [ju`naɪt] *v.* 聯合
   John and Sarah united forces to sign a big client for the firm.

2. **combine** [kəm`baɪn] *v.* 結合
   The organization is combining its Southeast and Northeast divisions to improve efficiency.

3. **existing** [ɪg`zɪstɪŋ] *adj.* 現有的
   We are planning to build a new skyscraper to replace our existing head office.

4. **receive** [rɪ`siv] *v.* 獲得
   At the award ceremony, attendees received a gift bag worth $100.

S: Smart. You're suggesting that by **combining**[2] our programs, we'd **bring the synergy*** between our brands **to bear**.

聰明。你的建議是結合我們的方案，我們能讓各自的品牌發揮協同效益。

K: Precisely.

沒錯。

A: I'm with you so far. However, I'm just not sure what extra value our customers get with Dash.

到目前為止我同意你所說的。但我只是不確定我們的顧客能透過飆風計畫得到什麼額外價值。

指「你說呢？」用於希望對方先提供意見的情況。

K: You tell me. What do your **existing**[3] programs offer?

你說呢？你們現有的方案提供了什麼？

A: Well, we provide discounts on set meals and allow for last-minute reservations.

嗯，我們提供套餐折扣並接受臨時訂位。

S: Our members **receive**[4] **exclusive**[5] promotions at different brand counters.

我們的會員在不同的品牌櫃位享有獨家的促銷優惠。

concession 讀做 [kən`sɛʃən]，指「優惠價格、減價」。

H: And ours get deals on concessions and can **trade in** their points for tickets or rewards.

我們的則有價格上的優惠，也能用點數折抵票券或獎品。

K: Fabulous. Dash would give shoppers access to all of that and more.

好極了。飆風計畫會提供顧客上述所有的好康，而且更多。

---

5. **exclusive** [ɪk`sklusɪv]
   adj. 獨家的；專屬的
   The credit card gives users exclusive access to our airport lounges around the world.

字彙補給站

* **ecosystem** [`iko͵sɪstəm] *n.* 生態圈

* **overlap** [`ovɚ͵læp] *n.* (顧客) 重疊

* **sector** [`sɛktɚ] *n.* 產業

* **synergy** [`sɪnɚdʒi] *n.* 綜效；協同作用

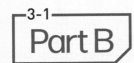

Part B 討論異業結盟

凱莉進一步解釋合作的好處，以加強提案的說服力。

K = Kelly   S = Sarah   H = Hector   A = Alex

K: I can tell by some of your faces that you're not completely **sold on** Dash. Give me a chance to **convince**[1] you.

我可以從你們一些人的臉上看出你們並沒有完全認同飆風計畫。給我個機會來說服你們。

S: Perhaps you could **elaborate**[2] on the ecosystem you mentioned.

也許你可以詳細説明你所提到的生態圈。

K: Sure. In concrete terms, I'm **referring**[3] to the pool of customers in our loyalty programs, which obviously would be far larger **were** we **to merge**[4] them.

當然。具體來説，我指的是我們各自酬賓方案中的客群，若將他們合併起來，肯定會多更多。

Vocabulary

1. **convince** [kən`vɪns] v. 說服
   Sheryl convinced her boss to give her a two-week extension on the project.

2. **elaborate** [ɪ`læbə‚ret]
   v. 詳細説明（＋on）
   The group elaborated on their research into the toy market.

3. **refer** [rɪ`fə] v. 提到；談及（＋to）
   Erica referred to the comments of the CEO in her news article.

H： And you believe this horizontal alliance would have a positive effect on our <u>bottom lines</u>?

> bottom line 指財報最後一行標示淨利或淨損的資訊，即「損益結算線」，後引申指「盈虧狀況」。

而你認為這個異業結盟會對我們的盈虧狀況帶來正面的影響？

K： Yes, on revenues and on marketing costs since it would help with customer retention, and we'd also be sharing the cost of a cooperative marketing strategy.

是的，在營收和行銷成本上都是，因為此結盟對留客率是有幫助的，而且我們也可以分攤合作行銷策略的成本。

S： Are there any other advantages you can point to?

你還能指出任何其他的好處嗎？

K： Yes. As is **evidenced**[5] in a survey we carried out, our collaboration would further our reach with customers that are not traditionally in our target demo.

可以。如我們進行的調查所顯示的，彼此的合作能延伸觸及以往不在我們目標客群中的顧客。

A： Makes sense. We each **appeal**[6] to different market segments. I can't **speak for** the others, but I'm <u>warming up to</u> the idea.

有道理。我們各自吸引不同的市場劃分區塊。我無法替其他人發言，但我開始喜歡這個想法了。

> warm up to 指「對……變得感興趣」。

---

4. **merge** [mɝdʒ] v. 合併；結合
   The movie studios plan to merge their businesses once they get approval from regulators.

5. **evidence** [ˋɛvədəns] v. 顯示；證明
   The popularity of the product was evidenced by the record-setting launch.

6. **appeal** [əˋpil] v. 吸引（＋to）
   The tech company's policies appeal to young professionals in their 20s and 30s.

Part C 協商成本分攤

凱莉向三人解釋結盟的成本規畫與分攤方式。

H = Hector　　K = Kelly　　A = Alex　　S = Sarah

H: I'm **curious**[1] to know how much this is going to cost.

我好奇地想知道這將會花多少錢。

K: The Shore Hotel **is deeply invested in** Dash. We're willing to **pick up the tab** to design the app and card as well as manufacture the first run of Dash cards.

濱海飯店傾注全力於飆風計畫中。我們願意掏錢來設計應用程式和卡片,以及生產第一輪的飆風卡。

A: That's very **generous**[2] of your organization. What would you need from us?

你們公司非常慷慨。你需要我們做什麼呢?

Vocabulary

1. **curious** [ˈkjʊriəs] *adj.* 好奇的
   Norman is very curious and always asks lots of interesting questions.

2. **generous** [ˈdʒɛnərəs] *adj.* 慷慨的
   It was very generous of you to take us out for dinner tonight.

3. **cover** [ˈkʌvɚ] *v.* 支付
   The supplier will cover the shipping costs if we order 5,000 units.

K： We're asking that you three **cover**[3] the material costs, about $6,000 in total, to begin with.

> 可用於話題轉換時，指「至於……；說到……」。

我們需要你們三方一開始時負擔材料成本，總共約六千美元。

S： That's fair. <u>As for</u> the marketing costs, I think a four-way split is **called for**, don't you?

那很合理。至於行銷成本，我認為四方均分是需要的，你們覺得呢？

H： I have no **objections**[4] to that. We all **benefit**[5] equally from the promotional materials after all.

我對那點沒有異議。畢竟我們都同樣從這些宣傳工具中獲益。

A： That means each of us would need to **put in**[6] an additional $9,000. I believe we can <u>make that work</u>.

> make sth work 指「使某事可行、運作得起來」。

那表示我們各方得投入額外的九千美元。我相信我們可讓此計畫運作起來的。

K： I understand you all are **taking a leap of faith** here, but I promise it will be worth it in the end.

我知道你們都是放手一搏，但我保證最後會是值得的。

---

4. **objection** [əb`dʒɛkʃən] *n.* 反對；異議
   People raised some objections to the city council about the redevelopment plan.

5. **benefit** [ˋbɛnəfɪt]
   v. 從……獲益（＋from）
   The firm benefited from the free advertisement generated by the viral video.

6. **put in** *v.* 投注（金錢、時間）
   Brenda and I each put in $15 for a subscription to the streaming service.

重點筆記

1. *put forward* 提出（意見、想法）

說明	此片語指「提出……建議、計畫等做為參考」，替換用法有 propose、bring up。

- The developer put forward a proposal to build a condo on the abandoned lot.
  該開發商提案要在廢棄空地上蓋一棟公寓。

2. *capitalize on* 從……中獲利

說明	動詞 capitalize [ˋkæpətəˏlaɪz] 指「資本化」，capitalize on sth 則表示「將某事物轉化為資本」，可引申形容「利用某事物、處境；從某事物中獲利」。

- Many celebrities are capitalizing on the popularity of live streaming.
  許多名人從直播的流行中獲利。

3. *bring sth to bear* 運用某事物

說明	此用語表示「帶來（ bring ）某事物，使予以承擔（ bear ）」，進而「發揮一定的效用或結果」，也就是「運用……、施加於……」的意思。

- The company brought maximum pressure to bear on the union, forcing them to accept the conditions.
  公司全力施壓於工會，迫使他們接受條件。

4. *trade in* 折抵；以……換取

說明	這個片語在商業領域中通常用來表示拿一樣舊的東西，加上一定金額後，換購新的東西回來，例如買新車時用舊車來折抵部分應付的金額。

- Every three years, I trade in my current car for a new model.
  每三年我就會將手上的車子折價換購為新款的。

5. *be sold on* 接受、認同……

說明	此慣用語常用於因被説服而「接受、贊同」某事物的情況。

- I'm sold on Cory's idea to redesign our company logo.
  我認同寇瑞重新設計公司標誌的想法。

6. *were ... to ...* 若……

說明	were . . . to . . . 為 if 假設語氣的變化句式,用於假設「如果某人做某事的話」,未來就可以達到某結果。

- Were we to leave now, we might arrive on time for the event.
  若我們現在離開,或許就能準時抵達活動現場。

7. *speak for sb* 代表某人發言

說明	speak for sb 表示「代表某人發言、表達意見」,相關用法的 speak for oneself 則以字面義「(事實)為自己説話」引申指「不言自明;不言而喻」。

- Robert doesn't speak for all of us, and I don't agree with his argument.
  羅伯特並不代表我們所有人發言,而且我不同意他的論點。

- The facts of the case speak for themselves, so the defendant is clearly guilty.
  這個案子的事實足以説明一切,因此被告顯然有罪。

8. *be deeply invested in* 傾盡全力於……

說明	此片語形容花了很多時間和精力去做某事,並且投注相當的在意程度。

- William is deeply invested in his start-up and wants it to turn a profit.
  威廉傾盡全力於他的新創公司並希望能獲利。

9. *pick up the tab* 承擔費用

說明	the tab [tæb] 指「待付的帳單、帳款」，整個用法即指「負擔某費用」。

- The boss will pick up the tab for the company trip.
  老闆將負擔員工旅遊的費用。

10. *call for* 需要

說明	call for 在英文中的常見用法有：

Ⓐ 需要（對話用法）
- This job calls for excellent customer service skills and attention to detail.
  這份工作需要絕佳的客服本領和細心度。

Ⓑ 呼喊
- I called for Adam's attention, but he didn't hear me.
  我呼喊要引起亞當的注意，但是他沒聽到。

Ⓒ 公開呼籲；訴求
- The union is calling for better working conditions at the manufacturing facilities.
  工會訴求生產廠房應有更好的工作環境。

11. *take a leap of faith* 放手一搏

說明	leap [lip] 指「跳躍」，faith [feθ] 指「信念」，此用法以字面義「踏出信心之躍」來表示「在不確定的情況下憑著信心而行」，意近中文的「放手一搏」。

- Both decisions present their own risks, so we just have to take a leap of faith.
  兩個決定各有風險，所以我們只得放手一搏。

延伸學習

行銷小百科

loyalty program

[ˋlɔɪəltɪ] 酬賓計畫

透過紅利集點方式來鼓勵顧客長期於該商家進行消費的促銷手法，以此加深顧客對品牌或企業的忠誠度，進而創造穩定的獲利。

horizontal alliance

[ˏhɔrəˋzɑntl̩] 異業結盟

指不同類型的產業，為擴大其規模、提升市占率或提高信息和資源共用力度而組成的利益共同體。

customer retention

[rɪˋtɛnʃən] 顧客保留

此概念在於留住現有顧客，方法是利用量身訂製的產品或服務來提升顧客滿意度與忠誠度，以創造延續性的獲利。

market segment

[ˋsɛgmənt] 市場劃分區塊

將個人或機構客戶，按照各自特點分類所得出的結果，使每個類別具有相似的產品服務需求。

target demo

[ˋtɑrgət] [ˋdɛmo] 目標客群

demo 為 demographic「人口族群」的縮寫，而目標客群指的是企業欲獲得的客戶族群。

3-2 Proposing a Strategic Alliance
合作提案 II

提案實用句 PLAY ALL

基本介紹

- For those of you who may not know me, I'm Kyle Donahue, senior engineer here at Time Trial.

  你們有人可能不認識我,我是凱爾‧唐納修,時淬公司的資深工程師。

- We're happy to have this opportunity to show you why KMO is your logical choice for precision prototype tooling.

  我們很高興有這個機會向你們介紹,為何 KMO 公司是貴司在精密原型模具上的合理選擇。

- PR Elite is the largest public relations firm in the region, and we've already handled over 30 successful corporate transitions.

  PR 菁英公司是本地區最大的公關公司,而且我們已成功處理了超過三十件的企業轉型案子。

競爭優勢

- We're trusted for **our flexible design capabilities and optimized facilities.**

  我們以彈性的設計能力和優化的設備而深受信賴。

- We have more than **50 specialists** who can provide **extremely cost-effective solutions.**

  我們有超過五十名專員可提供極具成本效益的解決方案。

- We're experts at **advanced 3D printing and precision CNC machining.**

  我們是先進 3D 列印和精密電腦數值控制加工的專家。

承諾貢獻

- We will target the specific demographics that would be the most interested in what you have to offer.

  我們將鎖定對貴司產品可能會最有興趣的特定消費族群。

- We'll be able to give your company exactly what it needs to increase sales.

  我們將能提供貴司確切所需以提高銷售。

- We will make the **Convex** name synonymous with **rapid prototyping.**

  我們將讓康維克斯的名字成為快速模型的同義詞。

Part A 向客戶提案

公關公司 PR 之星的奈德（Ned）和貝蒂（Betty）向到訪的客戶進行公司簡介，希望能贏得合作機會……

N = Ned   B = Betty   W = Wes

N: Thank you very much for coming today. We appreciate your time. For those of you who may not know me, I'm Ned Taylor, senior accounts director here at PR Star. We're happy to have this opportunity to show you at NorCal Tablets why PR Star is the only **logical**[1] choice for your transition from ODM to OBM. But first, I'd like to introduce my colleague, Betty Miller, public relations director.

非常謝謝你們今天的范臨。我們很感謝你們願意撥出時間。你們有人可能不認識我，我是奈德・泰勒，PR 之星的資深客戶總監。我們很高興有這個機會向諾卡平板電腦的各位介紹，為何 PR 之星是貴司從 ODM 轉型為 OBM 的唯一合理選擇。但首先，我想先介紹我的同事，貝蒂・米勒，她是公關總監。

Vocabulary

1. **logical** [ˋlɑdʒɪkəl] *adj.* 合理的
It's only logical that if you paid for lunch last time, I should buy it this time.

2. **hesitate** [ˋhɛzəˌtet] *v.* 猶豫；躊躇
Phil hesitated before asking Carl to help him finish the project.

B: This is an informal presentation, so if you have any questions, please don't **hesitate**[2] to **speak up**.

PR Star is the largest public relations firm in the region, and we've already handled several **high-profile**[3] ODM to OBM transitions. We're trusted for our tailored, unique <u>approaches</u> to raising brand awareness.

approach 讀做 [əˋprotʃ]，指「方法、方式」。

N: Our public information specialists are the best. We have more than 40 PR **gurus**[4] who can handle all of your earned and paid media needs.

W: How do we know you will **get** NorCal's voice **across** to the public?

N: Betty would be more qualified to answer that question. Betty?

B: Think of us as your creative partner. We will target the specific demographics that would be the most interested in what you have to offer, like mobile users.

這是非正式的簡報，所以你們有任何問題的話，請不要遲疑，儘管說出來。

PR 之星是本地區最大的公關公司，而且我們已處理了好幾件從 ODM 轉型為 OBM 的知名案子。我們以量身打造的獨特方法來提高品牌知名度而深受信賴。

我們的公共信息專員是最優秀的。我們有超過四十名公關專家可處理貴司所有的賺得媒體和付費媒體需求。

我們如何知道你們會將諾卡的信息傳達給大眾？

貝蒂更適合回答那個問題。貝蒂？

把我們想成是你們的創意夥伴。我們將鎖定對貴司產品可能會最有興趣的特定消費族群，例如手機使用者。

---

3. **high-profile** [haɪˋproˌfaɪl]
   adj. 受矚目的
   The company wanted a high-profile speaker at the conference in order to impress customers.

4. **guru** [ˋguru] *n.* 專家；權威
   Many fashion gurus write blogs about their opinions of the latest trends.

Part B 討論宣傳策略

諾卡平版電腦公司的威斯（Wes）
和珍（Jen）向奈德及貝蒂說明他們
期望能藉由公關公司的宣傳來提高
品牌知名度……

W = Wes   J = Jen   B = Betty   N = Ned

W: Thank you for such an **enlightening**[1] introduction to your firm.

> 讀做 [plʌs]，指「好處、優勢」。

謝謝你們如此具啟發性的公司
介紹。

J: We have a limited budget for paid media, so it's a <u>plus</u> for us that PR Star has such diverse contacts in the media.

我們在付費媒體的預算有限，
所以 PR 之星在媒體有如此多
樣化的門路，對我們來說有加
分效果。

W: True. We don't want to be **left high and dry when it comes to** media exposure, otherwise our transition would never **get off the ground.**

沒錯。我們不想在媒體曝光這
方面顯得孤立無援，否則我們
的轉型永遠無法順利展開。

Vocabulary

1. **enlightening** [ɪnˈlaɪtnɪŋ]
   adj. 啟發性的
   The professor gave an enlightening speech on ancient cultures.

2. **maximize** [ˈmæksəˌmaɪz] *v.* 最大化
   We maximize profits by keeping expenses in check.

J: I also like your plan to appeal to **tech-savvy** consumers. That's where the <u>big money</u> is.

> 指「大筆的錢」，意同 large sums of money。

我也很喜歡你們吸引科技通消費者的計畫。那是龐大商機所在。

B: We'll be able to give your company exactly what it needs to increase sales. We're experts at **maximizing**[2] public exposure while **minimizing**[3] costs.

我們將能提供貴司確切所需以提高銷售。我們是能最大化公眾曝光率且同時最小化成本的專家。

N: As our client, you would **have access to** all the resources you need to make a smooth transition without **breaking the bank**.

做為我們的客戶，你們可享有不必花大錢就能順利轉型的全部所需資源。

B: We will make the NorCal name **synonymous**[4] with superior tablets.

我們將讓諾卡的名字成為高級平板電腦的同義詞。

J: I'm impressed.

> 讀做 [ˋɪʃu]，於此為動詞，指「發布、發表」。

真令我印象深刻。

W: As am I. We want to <u>issue</u> a press release in four weeks. Can you have one ready by then?

我也是。我們想要在四週內發新聞稿。你們在那之前能準備好嗎？

N: Absolutely. In fact, we **took the liberty of** drawing up one **in case** everything went well today.

當然。事實上，想說倘若今天一切都進行得很順利，我們就逕自草擬了一份新聞稿。

W: Looks great. I think we've found our PR firm!

看起來很棒。我想我們找到公關公司了！

---

3. **minimize** [ˋmɪnəˌmaɪz] v. 使減到最少
   Megan minimized her tax bill by shifting money into a retirement account.

4. **synonymous** [səˋnɑnəməs] adj. 同義的
   Paris is synonymous with elegance and style.

重點筆記

1. *speak up* 暢所欲言

說明	speak up 的字面義為「大聲說話」，在此則指「直言表達看法」，與 speak out 意思相同，常用 speak up for + N. 或 speak out against + N. 來表示「公開支持／反對……」。

- Louis spoke up in meetings about buying new computers.
  路易斯在會議中發表添購新電腦的意見。

- Earl spoke up for his friend who was cheated by a crooked businessman.
  厄爾替他那被黑心商人騙的朋友出頭。

2. *get across* 傳達；表達

說明	get across 在英文中的常見用法有：

Ⓐ 傳達；表達（對話用法）

Max got his point across with the help of a PowerPoint presentation.
麥克斯藉由 PowerPoint 簡報軟體來傳達他的論點。

Ⓑ 越過；渡過

To get across the river, you should use the bridge.
你需要用這座橋來渡河。

3. *(be) left high and dry* 陷入困境

說明	以船隻行駛中碰上海水退潮，擱淺在高出水面的陸地上而動彈不得的意象，比喻遭遇困難卻無人援助的窘境，即「孤立無援；深陷困境」之意。對話中則為被動用法。

- The new trade agreement has left local farmers high and dry.
  新的貿易協定使當地農民陷入困境。

4. when it comes to 談到……

說明	when it comes to 為慣用語，表示「說到；提到……」，而由於 to 在此是介系詞，所以後面必須接名詞或 V-ing。

- When it comes to **meeting deadlines, we can never seem to find enough time.**
  談到在期限內完成工作，我們的時間似乎總是不夠。

5. get off the ground （活動、事業等）順利開展

說明	此語原指飛行時剛離開地面要起飛，亦常用來形容事物「順利開展」。

- Without a loan from the bank, this project will never get off the ground.
  沒有銀行的貸款，這個計畫將永遠無法順利開展。

6. tech-savvy 精通科技的

說明	savvy [ˋsævɪ] 指「通曉的；有見識的」，前面可加名詞來構成複合形容詞，表示「對……通曉的」。對話中的 tech-savvy「通曉科技的」即由 tech（technology）和 savvy 組成。來看看其他應用：
	
	computer + ⎫
	          ⎬ -savvy
	   media + ⎭
	
	= computer-savvy 通曉電腦的
	= media-savvy 通曉媒體的

- Rudy was the most computer-savvy person in the office.
  魯迪是辦公室裡最懂電腦的人。

7. *have access to* 有辦法使用

說明	access [ˈækˌsɛs] 當名詞指「使用權；接觸機會」。對話中的 have access to + N. 指「有辦法使用、接觸到某人事物」。

- I have access to a car this weekend because my brother is letting me use his.
  我這週末有辦法用車，因為我哥允許我用他的車。

8. *break the bank* 花大錢

說明	這個說法最早出現在賭博遊戲中，用來表示玩家贏了很多錢，多到連莊家（ the banker ）都付不出來，也就是使莊家破產的意思，後來漸漸被用來表示「花很多錢；透支」。

- The cost of car repairs can really break the bank.
  汽車修理費用可能會非常可觀。

9. *take the liberty of* 自行作主……；擅自……

說明	liberty [ˈlɪbɜtɪ] 可指「自由權；未經許可的行為」，take the liberty of 即表示「某人擅自（做某事）」。

- I took the liberty of borrowing your lawn mower while you were away.
  你不在的時候，我擅自借了你的除草機。

10. *in case* 以備；以防

說明	in case 用來表示為可能發生的事做準備，可放在句中或句首，後面可接子句或 of + N.。

- You should bring some extra money with you in case there is an emergency.
  你應該多帶點錢以備急用。

延伸學習

品牌小詞典

original equipment manufacturer (OEM)
原始設備製造商（代工）

通常譯做「原始設備製造商」或「專業代工」。由採購方提供技術，製造商依其需求製成產品，而後掛上客戶的商標品牌，由客戶自行銷售。

original design manufacturer (ODM)
原始設計製造商

一般譯為「原始設計製造商」或「委託設計製造商」。即製造商依採購方的需求，從設計到生產一手包辦，之後再由採購方以其商標品牌（trademark/logo）進行產品銷售。ODM 與 OEM 最大的不同點在於 ODM 廠商具備設計能力與技術。

own branding & manufacturing (OBM)
自有品牌生產

生產商建立自有品牌，從設計、採購、生產、行銷到販售，皆獨力完成。

brand awareness
品牌識別度

品牌被消費者認識或識別的能力，是關係到消費者購買與否的要素，也是品牌發展策略的關鍵因素。

earned media
賺得媒體

能使消費者自動產生口碑、評價的媒體，如 Facebook、Twitter 等社交網站。

paid media　付費媒體

向媒體付費以取得傳遞訊息的時間和空間，如電視廣告、網路橫幅廣告等。一般常用的行銷模式是利用付費媒體來接觸大量陌生客戶，再依靠對產品感到滿意的消費者來形成賺得媒體，以擴大行銷的成效。

3-3 Boasting about a Company

突顯競爭優勢

說明公司競爭優勢必備句  PLAY ALL

競爭優勢

We pride ourselves on . . .
我們對於⋯⋯感到自豪。

· We pride ourselves on having the best equipment in the industry.
我們對於擁有業界最優良的設備感到自豪。

Our products are enjoyed by . . .
我們的產品廣受⋯⋯的喜愛。

· Our products are enjoyed by loyal customers in more than 130 countries worldwide.
我們的產品廣受世界各地一百三十多國忠實顧客的喜愛。

By (year), we had become . . .
到了（年分），我們已成為⋯⋯

· By 2019, we had become the top chip manufacturer in Asia.
到了 2019 年，我們已成為亞洲頂尖的晶片製造商。

公司信譽

As . . ., we have a reputation to uphold.
做為……，我們必須要維護信譽。

· As the largest vitamin supplement supplier in the country, we have a reputation to uphold.
做為國內最大的維他命補給品供應商，我們必須要維護信譽。

We are esteemed for . . .
我們因……而備受敬重。

· We are esteemed for our honesty and integrity.
我們因誠信而備受敬重。

企業前景

We hope to become . . .
我們期望能成為……

· We hope to become a well-respected brand in beauty products.
我們期望能成為美容產品所備受推崇的品牌。

Our future plans will be focused on . . .
我們未來的計畫將著重在……

· Our future plans will be focused on increasing our market share in Europe.
我們未來的計畫將著重在增加我們的歐洲市占率。

Our vision is. . .
我們的願景是……

· Our vision is to open 15 new chain stores each year in countries around the world.
我們願景是每年在世界各國開設十五家新的連鎖店。

 **Part A** 說明公司運作

尚恩（Sean）向凱莉（Carrie）和布萊德（Brad）介紹其廠房的運作方式⋯⋯

S = Sean   C = Carrie   B = Brad

S: Hello, Carrie and Brad. It's a pleasure to finally meet you face-to-face.

C: Likewise.

S: Do you have any questions for me before we begin the tour of our facilities?

B: Yes. After the fruits and vegetables are gathered, how long until they are sent to your distributors?

哈囉，凱莉和布萊德。很高興終於和你們見面了。

我們也一樣。

我們開始參觀設備之前，你們有什麼問題要問我的嗎？

有的。蔬果採收後多久會送到你們的經銷商那裡？

Vocabulary

1. **inspect** [ɪnˋspɛkt] *v.* 檢查
   To be sure there were no errors, the boss would inspect every outgoing e-mail.

2. **overlook** [ˌovɚˋluk] *v.* 忽略；看漏
   Pam overlooked an important detail on her résumé.

3. **sustainable** [səˋstenəbəl] *adj.* 永續的；能長期維持的
   The current production rate is not sustainable with a smaller staff.

S: Once the farmers **drop off** their crops at our warehouse, Quality Control **inspects**[1] them. It's a step in the process that many of our competitors seem to **overlook**.[2] As the top **sustainable**[3] organic supplier in the country, we have a **reputation**[4] to **uphold**.[5] Therefore, every crate is inspected manually before it's handed off to the distributors.

C: That must keep quite a few inspectors **occupied**![6]

S: It does, and we **pride ourselves on** having the finest ones in the industry.

B: Do those checks ever affect delivery schedules?

S: Our products are consistently sent out on schedule. Competitive prices, fresh organic foods, happy customers; that's what we aim for.

B: How many warehouses do you have?

S: Three here and another four in Brazil. Go to the source, I always say.

B: Impressive. It looks like you guys are really **on to a good thing**.

一旦農夫把作物送到我們的倉庫，品管人員就會進行檢查。過程中的這個步驟是我們許多競爭對手似乎都會忽略的。做為國內頂尖的永續有機供應商，我們必須要維護信譽。因此，每箱農產品在交給經銷商以前，都會經過人工檢查。

那一定讓不少檢查人員忙個不停吧！

的確，而我們對於擁有業界最優秀的檢查人員感到自豪。

那些檢查作業曾影響到運送時程嗎？

我們的產品一向都準時運送出去。具競爭力的價格、新鮮的有機食品以及滿意的顧客，這些都是我們的目標。

你們有多少間倉庫呢？

這裡有三間，另外四間在巴西。我總是說要直達產區。

真令人印象深刻。看來你們經營得很成功。

---

4. **reputation** [ˌrɛpjəˈteʃən]
   n. 名聲；名譽
   Many celebrities' reputations have been damaged by the media.

5. **uphold** [ʌpˈhold] *v.* 維護
   The police are expected to uphold the law.

6. **occupied** [ˈɑkjəˌpaɪd]
   adj. 忙於……的
   Everyone in the office was fully occupied with work.

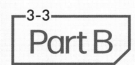

Part B 說明公司優勢

尚恩繼續向布萊德和凱莉說明其公司的沿革和營運方式……

B = Brad   S = Sean   C = Carrie

B: Thanks for all the info about what happens in your facilities. Would you mind also **filling us in** on your company's background a bit?

謝謝你告知貴司設備的所有運作情形。你能也告訴我們一些關於貴司的背景嗎？

S: I'd be happy to. Produce Fresh was founded in 1972. We **landed**[1] our first agriculture contract in 1975. By 1981, we had become the top organic supplier on the West Coast.

我很樂意。新鮮生產創立於 1972 年。我們在 1975 年拿下第一份農產品合約。到了 1981 年，我們已成為西岸的頂尖有機供應商。

C: You said you have seven warehouses. How many stores do you supply to?

你說你們有七間倉庫。那你們供應產品給多少家商店呢？

Vocabulary

1. **land** [lænd] *v.* 獲得；贏得
   Jeremy tried to land more business for his company, but he wasn't successful.

2. **employ** [ɪm`plɔɪ] *v.* 使用；利用
   Monica employed her knowledge of the industry to accurately predict future trends.

S: We deliver to 750 stores in North America every week. We hope to become the largest organic crop supplier in the world soon.

我們每週運送產品至北美的七百五十家商店。我們期望很快能成為全球最大的有機農產品供應商。

B: How do you **employ**[2] the latest technology in your process?

你們如何將最新的科技運用在加工流程中？

指「無奈接受；勉強同意」。

S: We refuse to <u>settle for</u> outdated tools. Besides our **state-of-the-art**[3] sorting and packing machines, we also **utilize**[4] amazing software on portable devices that can track every crate that enters our doors.

我們拒絕接受過時的器具。除了我們最先進的分類與包裝機具，我們也將很棒的軟體應用在可攜式裝置上，能追蹤進來的每箱產品。

C: Do you have any upgrades planned?

你們有任何升級的計畫嗎？

S: Our future improvements will really be focused on our overseas operations. Customers are demanding a more global variety of fruit, and we aim to offer exactly what they want.

我們未來的改善計畫將著重於海外的營運。消費者要求更具全球多樣性的水果，而我們計畫提供他們確切想要的。

C: Well, it seems like Produce Fresh is really **going places**. I look forward to our tour through this warehouse so I can really see what's going on with my own eyes.

嗯，看來新鮮生產真的很成功。我期待參觀這整座倉庫，以便親眼看看運作的情形。

N: Absolutely. Let's get going. I have a lot to show you.

當然。我們走吧。我有很多東西要給你們看。

---

3. **state-of-the-art** [ˈstetəvˌðɪˈɑrt] *adj.* 最先進的
The engineer is helping to design a state-of-the-art skyscraper.

4. **utilize** [ˈjutəˌlaɪz] *v.* 應用
To succeed in this competitive business world, one needs to utilize one's abilities.

重點筆記

1. *drop off* 留下；讓……下車

說明	drop off 在此意同 drop，表示「將貨物中途卸貨；讓乘客中途下車」。

- I will drop the dry cleaning off on my way to work and pick it up on the way home.
  我上班途中會把乾洗的衣物送去，回家時再去拿。
- The bus dropped off four of the passengers at a bus stop near the lake.
  公車在湖邊的一處站牌讓四名乘客下車。

2. *pride oneself on sth* 自豪於……

說明	pride 在此當動詞，指「使得意；使感到驕傲」，pride oneself 則指「感到自傲；自豪」，後面些 on 來帶出引以為傲的事物。相似用法為 take pride in sb/sth「對某人事物感到驕傲」。

- The company prides itself on producing quality, low-cost cars.
  該公司以製造優質且低價的車子而自豪。

3. *on to a good thing* 方向正確；進行順利

說明	指一件事所進行的方向正確，正朝著想要的結果推進。類似用法為 on the right track。

- I think Kyle is on to a good thing with his environmentally-friendly business practices.
  我覺得凱爾的環保經營方式方向正確。
- The company is on the right track with its new sales plan.
  該公司的新銷售計畫前景看好。

4. *fill in* 提供資訊

說明	fill in 在英文中的常見用法有：

ⓐ 提供更多資訊（對話用法）

As you were absent from the meeting yesterday, I'll fill you in on what was decided.
因為你昨天沒出席會議，我再告訴你決議的內容。

ⓑ 填寫

Please fill in this form with all your personal information.
請在這張表格填寫您所有的個人資料。

ⓒ 暫替；暫代

Since Jared had called in sick, the boss asked Darren to fill in for him.
因為傑瑞德打來說他生病了，老闆就叫達倫暫代他的工作。

ⓓ 填補（不足的地方）

Jane's autobiographical essay filled in the blanks about her mysterious past.
珍的自傳式散文填補了她神祕的過往。

5. *go places* 不斷進展

說明	字面上的意思是「去很多地方」，用來形容「獲得成功；有所成就」。相反詞則為 go nowhere，以字面義「哪裡都去不了」比喻「沒有前途」。

• After her big promotion, it seems that Gina is really going places.
高升之後，吉娜似乎真的有所成就了。

爭取代理權必備句 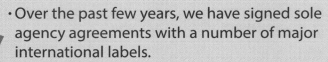 PLAY ALL

代理優勢

· Over the past few years, we have signed sole agency agreements with a number of major international labels.

過去幾年來，我們已和不少國際大品牌簽下獨家代理合約。

· A recent high point of our company was winning the exclusive rights to distribute French jewelry brand Bijou Bee's products in Taiwan.

我們公司近期最精采的事蹟是贏得法國珠寶品牌小蜜蜂產品的台灣獨家經銷權。

市場分析

· Based on our market research, we are confident that there is a gap in the market for this kind of product.

根據市調，我們有信心這類產品會有市場。

· With no competitors currently offering anything like this, there is undoubtedly an opportunity for us.

由於目前沒有競爭者提供任何這類的產品，對我們來說無疑是個機會。

行銷手法

- Using a targeted campaign, we will be focusing on the young, upwardly-mobile demographic.
藉由採用目標性的宣傳活動，我們將聚焦在年輕的上層社會族群。

- The intention is to employ a word-of-mouth approach through the use of social media influencers and opinion leaders.
此行銷手法意圖透過社群媒體影響者和意見領袖來善用口碑行銷。

銷售預測

- We believe a first-quarter projection in excess of NT$300,000 is a realistic target.
我們相信首季預期銷售額超過新台幣三十萬元是個實際的目標。

- While initial sales might be slow, things should pick up toward the end of the year following the introduction of our pop-up stores.
儘管初期的銷售可能緩慢，但快閃店推出後，到年底的銷售應該會拉高。

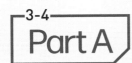 **Part A** 公司概況介紹

里歐（Leo）和譚美（Tammy）到韓國首爾與克莉絲汀（Christine）洽談品牌代理權。

L = Leo　　T = Tammy　　C = Christine

L： First off, we really appreciate you taking the time to meet.

首先，我們很感謝你抽空會面。

> 指「遠遠地」，意同 from a great distance。

T： It's a real honor. We've admired your work <u>from afar</u>, and now we're meeting the <u>legend</u> in person!

真的很榮幸。我們遠在台灣就已久仰你的作品，現在總算見到傳奇人物本尊了！

> 讀做 [ˈlɛdʒənd]，指「傳奇人物」。

Vocabulary

1. **represent** [ˌrɛprɪˈzɛnt] *v.* 代理；代表
We have hired someone in Taiwan to represent our company at this year's Computex.

2. **post** [post] *v.* 公布（消息）
Amazon posted its highest recorded profits ever at $1.9 billion in 2017.

C: Thanks for the kind words. I have to say, your e-mail piqued my interest.

謝謝你們的讚美。我得說,你們的來信引起我的興趣。

T: Good to hear. Let's start with a quick company intro.

很開心聽你這麼說。我們就以快速的公司介紹開始吧。

intro [ˈɪnˌtro] 是 introduction「介紹;簡介」的簡寫。

L: We've been a leader in the Taiwanese market for 20 years, **representing**[1] five Japanese brands and **posting**[2] sales of NT$120 million last year.

二十年來,我們一直是台灣市場的領導者,代理了五個日本品牌,去年的公告業績則是新台幣 1.2 億元。

C: Impressive figures.

了不起的數字。

讀做 [ˈkraʊnɪŋ],為形容詞,指「最重要的」。

T: Our crowning achievement is having the sole agency for Bloom at 10 counters in department stores across Taiwan.

我們最大的成就是獨家代理花綻品牌,在全台的百貨公司設立了十個櫃點。

L: Besides that, we have years of experience in online retail.

除此之外,我們有多年的線上零售經驗。

C: That's where the sales are nowadays.

那是現今的銷售場域。

L: And we're confident we can **replicate**[3] that success with your designs.

而我們有信心可藉由你的設計商品再複製那樣的成功。

---

3. **replicate** [ˈrɛpləˌket] v. 複製
Companies can have a hard time trying to replicate previous successes when they stop innovating.

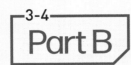

Part B 討論市場定位

克莉絲汀詢問譚美和里歐台灣的目標市場。

C = Christine   T = Tammy   L = Leo

C: Thanks for the background, but what I'm really **curious**[1] about is the market in Taiwan. I know **next to nothing** about <u>consumer behavior</u> there.

> 指「消費者行為」，涉及購買行為的所有方面，即從購買前的活動到購買後的消費、評價和處理活動。

謝謝你們的背景介紹，但我真正好奇的是台灣的市場。我對當地的消費者行為幾乎一無所知。

T: Right. Well, the demand for handmade items has **gone through the roof** recently.

好的。嗯，近來大眾對手工製品的需求激增。

Vocabulary

1. **curious** [ˈkjuriəs]
adj. 好奇的（+ about）
Sheryl is very curious about what the research and development department is currently working on.

2. **cater** [ˈketɚ] *v.* 迎合（+ to）
Luxury brands like Rolex and Chanel cater to the rich and famous.

L: And the current penchant* for <u>all things</u> Korean —

> all things + adj. 指「所有關於⋯⋯的一切」。

T: — which is to say, dramas, K-pop, and fashion —

L: Well, that makes this a **no-brainer**. When people in Taiwan think "Korean," they think "trendy."

C: Interesting. So what kind of demographic would you be looking at? Here, my designs **cater**[2] mainly to consumers in their early 20s.

T: So we've heard. I think we'd be looking at an older crowd* with more <u>disposable wealth</u> — the 25 to 35 bracket.*

> disposable wealth [dɪˋspozəbəl] 指「可支配財富」，另一常見的 disposable in come 指「可支配所得」。

還有當前大家對所有韓國相關事物的偏愛——

也就是韓劇、韓國流行樂以及時尚。

嗯，那種現況讓這個合作不用多想。當台灣人想到「韓系」，就會想到「時尚」。

很有意思。所以你們要鎖定的是哪類族群？在這裡，我的設計主要迎合二十出頭的消費者。

我們聽說了。我想我們會鎖定有更多可支配財富的稍長族群——25 到 35 歲這個區間。

字彙補給站

* **penchant** [ˋpɛntʃənt] *n.* 偏愛
* **crowd** [kraʊd] *n.* 群眾
* **bracket** [ˋbrækət] *n.* 區間

Part C 討論品牌行銷

接著，克莉絲汀想了解里歐和譚美的行銷手法。

C = Christine　　L = Leo　　T = Tammy

C: So we know who we're selling to. What can you tell me about how you intend to **get the brand message across**?

所以我們知道銷售對象了。關於你們打算如何傳遞品牌訊息，有什麼可以告訴我的嗎？

L: Well, let me answer your question with one of my own. What has your approach been here in Korea?

嗯，讓我用我自己的問題來回答你。你在韓國用的方法是什麼？

C: I think I'm **catching your drift**. <u>Product placement</u>?

我想我明白你的意思了。產品置入？

> 指「產品置入」，又稱 placement marketing「置入性行銷」。

Vocabulary

1. **tactic** [ˋtæktɪk] *n.* 手法；策略
The government is looking for tactics to slow the rising price of health care.

2. **generate** [ˋdʒɛnəˏret] *v.* 造成；產生
Viral marketing can be an innovative way to generate interest in a brand if done properly.

T: That would certainly be one **tactic**.[1] We've seen the buzz* **generated**[2] by having K-drama idols wear your designs.

那絕對是個手法。我們看見讓韓劇偶像配戴你的設計商品所造成的熱潮。

L: But we're pursuing a multipronged* strategy — one which would also **incorporate**[3] viral marketing. Vloggers, bloggers, social media . . .

但我們追求的是多管齊下的策略——其中也包含病毒式行銷。影音部落客、部落客、社群媒體……

• vlogger 為 video「影像」和 blogger「部落客」的混成詞，指「影音部落客」。

指「病毒式行銷」，是以網路社群和各種媒體管道發布訊息來吸引大眾對品牌、產品或活動的關注。

T: Live-streaming events where accessories worn in K-dramas are unboxed and the purchase details are displayed.

直播開箱介紹韓劇角色所配戴的飾品，並秀出購買資訊。

unbox 以字面義「拆箱」代表時下的網路用語「開箱」。

C: I like it. You guys have certainly **thought this through**.

我很喜歡。你們肯定認真思考過了

---

3. **incorporate** [ɪnˋkɔrpəˏret] *v.* 包含
Multinational corporations are beginning to incorporate community outreach into their mission statements and business models.

字彙補給站

＊ **buzz** [bʌz] *n.* 熱潮

＊ **multipronged** [ˏmʌltiˋprɔŋd] *adj.* 多方面的

業績預測

PLAY ALL ● TRACK 25

最後，克莉絲汀提出關於銷售管道和預估業績的問題。

C = Christine   T = Tammy   L = Leo

C: I was <u>wondering</u> what kind of channels* you'd **envisaged**[1] using.

> wonder 指「疑惑；想知道」，這裡搭配過去式的 was 是為表達「委婉的語氣」。

我想知道你們預計使用哪類銷售管道。

T: **With that in mind**, we've prepared this visual presentation for you.

考慮到這一點，我們為你準備了投影片。

Vocabulary

1. **envisage** [ɪnˈvɪzɪdʒ] *v.* 預計；展望
   Based on current trends, economists envisage a faster transition to renewable energy than thought before.

2. **optimistic** [ˌɑptəˈmɪstɪk] *adj.* 樂觀的
   Market speculators are optimistic that prices in the stock market will continue to rise this year.

原指「運行、運轉」，在此指「現時可行的；已開始進行的」。

L: If you look at the first column,* we've listed the channels. Online sales will be <u>up and running</u> **from the get-go** and will obviously be a <u>permanent fixture</u>.

請看第一欄，我們列出了銷售管道。網路銷售將從一開始就進行，且顯然會是長久的型態。

指「成為長久的型態」。permanent [ˋpɝmənənt]
指「長久的」，fixture [ˋfɪkstʃə] 則指「固定裝置」。

C: NT$300,000 per quarter. Is that not **optimistic**?[2]

每季新台幣三十萬元的業績。那不會太樂觀了嗎？

T: We don't think so.

我們不這麼認為。

C: OK. It looks like you have some pop-up stores **in the works**?

好的。你們看起來好像在準備幾間快閃店？

L: Those would be introduced in the first year in two phases.*

那會在第一年，分兩階段推出。

T: Finally, there are the department store spots, with a goal of three per year.

最後會有百貨公司櫃點，目標是每年設立三個。

C: I'm sold. I think we can start discussing terms.*

我被說服了。我想我們可以開始談合約條件了。

字彙補給站

* **channel** [ˋtʃænl̩] n. 管道
* **column** [ˋkɑləm] n. 欄位
* **phase** [fez] n. 階段
* **terms** [tɝmz] n. 條件

重點筆記

1. *next to nothing* 幾乎沒有

說明	此語以「在無物旁邊」的字面義形容「幾乎沒有；非常少」。相似拼法的 **next to last** 則指「倒數第二的」。

- I used to know next to nothing about investments until I worked at a bank.
  直到我在銀行工作之前，我對投資幾乎一無所知。

- Andrew finished next to last in the race.
  安德魯在比賽中排名倒數第二。

2. *go through the roof* 飆升

說明	此俚語以「衝破屋頂」的誇飾義形容「飛漲；激增」，另可指「火冒三丈、暴跳如雷」。

- Oil and gas prices are going through the roof as a result of recent sanctionson Russia.
  由於近期俄羅斯所受到的制裁，原油和天然氣的價格飆升。

- My parents went through the roof when they saw my report card.
  我父母看到我的成績單時氣壞了。

3. *no-brainer* 不費吹灰之力的事

說明	以字面義「不用動腦」來比喻「不費腦筋就可以處理的事」。

- If it's cold, wear a coat! That should be a no-brainer.
  如果天氣很冷，就穿上外套吧！這應該是連想都不用想的事。

4. *get sth across* 傳遞……；使……被理解

說明	此片語指「使被理解；使被傳達；把……說清楚」，常搭配 message、point 等字使用。

- The speaker tried to get his message across to the audience by repeating the main points.
  該講者藉由複述要點來試著讓聽眾明白他的話。

5. *catch sb's drift* 明白某人的意思

說明	catch 指「理解；聽清楚」，drift 於此為名詞，指「大意；主旨」，整個片語也可說 get one's drift。

- Do you know what Matt is saying? I cannot catch his drift.
  你知道麥特在說什麼嗎？我不明白他的意思。

6. *think sth through* 認真思考某事

說明	此片語指「認真考慮；想透」，形容仔細考慮做某事所可能帶來的結果。

- Companies should think new policies through before implementing them to avoid unintended consequences.
  在實行新政策前，企業應認真思考，才能避免非預期的結果。

7. *with that in mind* 考慮到這一點

說明	源自 with sth in mind 的用法，表示「想好、考慮到某事物」。

- We don't have much time, so with that in mind, we should finish our meeting soon.
  我們沒多少時間，所以考慮到這一點，我們應盡快結束會議。

8. *from the get-go* 從一開始

說明	get-go 為口語用法，指「開端、開始」，**from the get-go** 即形容「從一開始」，get-go 可用 beginning、outset 等字替換。

- After joining our staff, Bonny has been an excellent employee from the get-go.
  加入我們的團隊後，邦尼從一開始就一直是傑出的員工。

- We never expected this project to be so successful from the outset.
  我們從未預期這個專案從一開始就如此成功。

9. *in the works* 準備中

說明	work 指「勞動；作業」，**in the works** 即形容「在籌備中；在完成中」。

- Plans to launch a new fashion line have been in the works for months.
  推出新時尚系列的計畫已準備好幾個月了。

10. *I'm sold.* 我被說服了。

說明	sold 在此指「被說服的」，整句表達出被對方打動之意。

A: How about I lower the unit price to $15?
　　我把單價降低到 15 美元如何？
B: Well, I'm sold.
　　嗯，我被說服了。

延伸學習

圖解代理權相關詞彙

competitor
[kəm`pɛtətɚ]
競爭者

sole agency agreement
獨家代理合約

exclusive right
[ɪk`sklusɪv]
專有權；專營權

pop-up store
[`pɑp͵ʌp]
快閃店

market research
市場調查

demographic
[͵dɛmə`græfɪk]
族群

campaign
[kæm`pen]
宣傳

projection
[prə`dʒɛkʒən]
預測

opinion leader
意見領袖

social media
社群媒體

influencer
[`ɪnfluənsɚ]
影響者

word of mouth
口碑

UNIT
4 / Introducing Your Products

介紹產品

A Perfect Product Launch
產品發表會 I

產品發表流程圖 & 必備句型 PLAY ALL

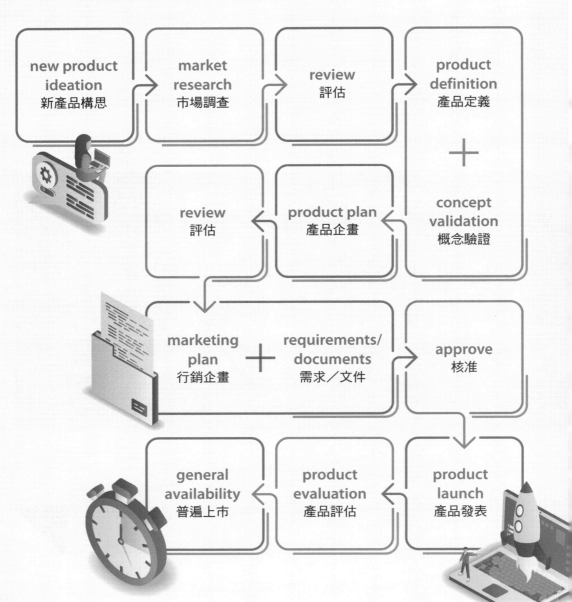

new product ideation 新產品構思 → market research 市場調查 → review 評估 → product definition 產品定義 + concept validation 概念驗證 → product plan 產品企畫 → review 評估 → marketing plan 行銷企畫 + requirements/documents 需求／文件 → approve 核准 → product launch 產品發表 → product evaluation 產品評估 → general availability 普遍上市

漂亮開場白

I'm excited to tell you all about (product/service).
我很高興要告訴你們所有關於（產品／服務）的事情。

· **I'm excited to tell you all about the new VT8 vacuum cleaner.**
我很高興要告訴你們所有關於新款 VT8 吸塵器的事情。

產品優勢

(Product/Service) takes (industry) to the next level.
（產品／服務）將（產業）帶往下一個層次。

· **The Sprint Hard treadmill takes fitness training to the next level.**
史賓哈德跑步機將健身訓練帶往下一個層次。

品質保證

Our top-notch team of specialists works around the clock to ensure . . .
我們頂尖的專家團隊日以繼夜地努力確保……

· **Our top-notch team of specialists works around the clock to ensure customer satisfaction.**
我們頂尖的專家團隊日以繼夜地努力確保顧客滿意度。

媒體廣宣

You'll be seeing a lot more of (product/ service) on . . .
各位將在……看到更多關於（產品／服務）的消息。

· **You'll be seeing a lot more of New City Electronics on major TV channels.**
各位將在各大電視頻道看到更多關於新城電子產品的消息。

Part A 介紹新產品

天際產業的行銷總監蘇（Sue）和研發部的經理華特（Walter）正在舉辦產品記者會……

S = Sue　　W = Walter

S: Hello! I'm so excited to see you all today. I'm even more excited to tell you all about Sky Industry's new Safe Storage System.

W: The Sky Safe Storage System **takes** cloud computing **to the next level**.

S: Imagine being able to **access**[1] all of your information anytime, anywhere.

worry 在此為名詞，指「令人擔心的事」。

W: No more <u>worries</u> about hard drives crashing. No more fears about losing precious data. Sky Safe Storage System's **got you covered**.

哈囉！我很高興今天見到在座的各位。我更高興地要告訴你們所有關於天際產業新安全儲存系統的事情。

天際安全儲存系統將雲端運算帶往下一個層次。

想像你能在任何時間、任何地點存取所有資訊。

不用再擔心硬碟毀損。不用再懼怕會失去珍貴數據。天際安全儲存系統提供你完整的保障。

Vocabulary

1. **access** [ˈækˌsɛs] v. 存取（資料）；使用
   I'm having trouble accessing the server at the moment.

2. **slogan** [ˈsloɡən] n. 廣告標語
   I still remember the slogan of my favorite candy bar when I was a kid.

S: Plus, the Sky Safe Storage System helps companies cut their IT costs.

此外，天際安全儲存系統可幫助公司行號削減資訊科技的成本。

W: That's why our service can best be **summed up** by the **slogan**[2] "Safe and Secure."

這也是為何我們的服務可用「安全且牢靠」的標語來完美概括。

S: Our **top-notch**[3] team of security specialists works **around the clock** to ensure the safety of your data.

我們頂尖的安檢專家團隊日以繼夜地努力確保諸位的數據安全。

> 讀做 [ˈdɛdəˌketəd]，指「盡心盡力的」，常用句型為 dedicated to + N./V-ing。

W: And we at Sky remain <u>dedicated</u> to keeping costs down, for both individuals and companies.

而天際的每個成員會繼續致力為個人和企業客戶降低成本。

S: See for yourself. Everyone here today gets six months of Sky Safe Storage System for free.

眼見為憑。今天，在場的各位都能免費使用六個月的天際安全儲存系統。

W: And anyone who **signs up for** Sky Safe Storage System this month gets the same.

而本月註冊天際安全儲存系統的任何人也能享有相同優惠。

S: You'll be seeing a lot more about this innovative system on Facebook and Twitter. And look for a special ad campaign on TV.

各位將在臉書和推特上看到更多關於此創新系統的消息。也請密切注意電視上的特別廣告活動。

W: **In the meantime**, if you have any questions about the Sky Safe Storage System, please let us know.

於此同時，若您對天際安全儲存系統有任何問題，請讓我們知道。

---

3. **top-notch** [ˈtɑpˈnɑtʃ] *adj.* 頂尖的
   To ensure the quality of our product, we only accept contracts with top-notch suppliers.

 **Part B** 提問與應答

蘇和華特回答在場各位記者的提問……

R1-5 = Reporter One to Five   S = Sue   W = Walter

R1: Can you guarantee that your users' information will be safe?

你們能保證用戶的資訊安全無虞嗎？

W: Thanks to Sky's **proprietary**[1] technology, all data stored in the Sky Safe Storage System will be secure.

由於天際的專利技術，所有儲存在天際安全儲存系統的資料都不會有安全上的問題。

R2: How is security kept **up to date**?

安全防護如何維持在最新版本？

S: Users receive free automatic updates to the system.

用戶享有免費自動更新系統的服務。

R3: What about other costs?

那其他費用呢？

Vocabulary

1. **proprietary** [prə`praɪəˌtɛrɪ] *adj.* 專利的
   We believe our proprietary blend of ingredients makes our health food items unique.

2. **accommodate** [ə`kɑməˌdet] *v.* 容納
   The hotel can accommodate up to 70 guests at a time.

S: You pay only for the amount of storage that you use.

你只須就你所使用的儲存量來付費。

W: So the Safe Storage System can **accommodate**[2] a few gigabytes of family photos or a few thousand terabytes of company data.

此安全儲存系統可容納數十億位元組的居家照片或數千太位元組的公司數據。

R4: Can you **clarify**[3] your pricing structure?

你們能說明你們的定價結構嗎？

S: Sure. Pricing is based on the amount of data stored, with discounts for larger amounts of data.

當然。售價是根據數據儲存量而定，更大量的數據則可享有優惠。

W: **In other words**, the more you store, the more you save.

也就是說，儲存越多，省的就越多。

R5: What about new technology? Will users be able to access their information with new devices?

關於新技術呢？用戶可藉由新裝置來存取他們的資料嗎？

S: Good question. As technology **evolves**,[4] Sky Safe Storage System will continue to evolve along with it.

問得好。隨著科技的發展，天際安全儲存系統將繼續隨之發展。

W: No matter if it's a computer, a server, a tablet, or even the next generation of smartphone, Sky Safe Storage System will **be there for you**.

無論是電腦、伺服器、平板電腦甚或是下一代的智慧型手機，天際安全儲存系統都會隨侍在側。

S: **The sky's the limit** with Sky Safe Storage System — and your data is always safe and secure.

天際安全儲存系統追尋無限可能——而你的數據永遠安全有保障。

---

3. **clarify** [ˈklɛrəˌfaɪ] v. 詳細說明
Could you please clarify what is meant by this section of the contract?

4. **evolve** [ɪˈvɑlv] v. 發展
The company started out selling beauty products but soon evolved into a fashion brand.

重點筆記

1. *take sth to the next level* 讓……更上一層樓

說明	字面義是「帶……到下一個層次、階段」，通常用來表示帶著已有的成果，更進一步地發展、進步，類似中文的「更上一層樓」。

- The new CEO took the company to the next level by pushing new and innovative products.
  新任執行長推動創新產品，讓公司更上一層樓。

2. *have (got) sb/sth covered* 提供完整的保障

說明	此慣用語形容已經完成、得到或提供所需的一切，即「處理好一切事物」。

- Don't worry about a thing. We've got you covered.
  別擔心。我們都幫你處理好了。

3. *sum up* 總結

說明	sum [sʌm] 做動詞指「總結；總計」，sum up 可具體地表示「（金額）總計」，也可抽象地指對某事物的「總結；摘要」。另一類似用法 to sum up 則指「總括來說、總而言之」，通常放句首，並用逗點和主要子句隔開。

- Mike summed up the future plans for the company at a meeting.
  麥克於會中為公司的未來計畫進行總結。

- To sum up, you need to work harder in order to be good at this job.
  總而言之，你得更努力才能勝任這份工作。

4. *around the clock* 不間斷地;不休息地

說明	以「繞著時鐘」的字面義引申指「日以繼夜地」,另一相似片語 against the clock 則指「分秒必爭地」。

- I've been working around the clock to meet this deadline.
  我日以繼夜地努力要趕上截止期限。

- It's a race against the clock to finish the designs ahead of the presentation.
  要在簡報前完成設計,真的得和時間賽跑。

5. *sign up for* 註冊;報名

說明	sign up 表示「報名;登記」,常接介系詞 for 來帶出所報名的項目。

- I signed up for the woodworking class at the community college.
  我報名了社區大學的木工課程。

6. *in the meantime* 於此同時;在此期間

說明	meantime 指「其時、其間」,in the meantime 則表示「於此同時;在此期間」,也可寫成 in the meanwhile。

- Welcome, everyone. The show will begin in five minutes. In the meantime, please turn off all your cellular devices.
  歡迎各位。表演將於五分鐘後開始。在此同時,請將您的手機都關機。

7. *up to date* 最新的;最近的

說明	up to date 指「最新的;最近的」,常搭配動詞 bring 和 keep。bring/keep sb up to date on/with + N. 即表示「讓某人掌握⋯⋯的最新訊息」。

- The event location might change. I'll keep you up to date if it does.
  活動地點可能變更。若更改的話,我會讓你知道最新消息。

8. *in other words* 換句話說

說明	形容用另一種方式陳述或解釋，多用於介紹、說明、簡化或澄清的情境。類似用法有 to put it another way、that is to say。

- Mr. Chan has another appointment on Friday. In other words, I don't think he'll be attending your gathering.
  詹先生星期五有別的行程。換句話說，我不認為他能參加你的聚會。

9. *be there for sb* 伴隨某人身旁

說明	此用法以字面義「為某人待在那裡」形容「總在某人身邊（提供幫助或支援）；不離某人左右」。

- Matthew and I haven't always been close, but he was there for me when I needed him.
  馬修和我並非總是很親密，但我需要他時，他都會在我身旁。

10. *the sky's the limit* 不可限量

說明	以「無邊無際的天空為限制」的意象來形容「什麼事都是有可能發生的」，若後面要接名詞，常會加上 for、with 等介系詞。

- With the development of artificial intelligence and machine learning, the sky's the limit.
  隨著人工智慧和機器學習的發展，一切都是有可能的。

延伸學習

產品發表好用詞 & 實用句

presenter 主持人
attendee 出席者
debut 初登場
positioning （產品的）定位

feasibility 可行性
available 可買到的
demonstration 示範說明
come in/with 具有⋯⋯／配備⋯⋯

Everyone was eagerly awaiting the video game system's debut.

每個人都殷切期盼該電玩系統的初登場。

The company relied heavily on market research when designing new products.

設計新產品時，該公司極度仰賴市場調查。

Strengthening the company's positioning in the new market was the CEO's primary concern.

強化公司在新市場的定位是執行長的主要考量。

Once the laptop became available, stores across the country sold out within a few days.

該筆記型電腦一上市，幾天內就在全國各地的商店完售。

The salesman gave a demonstration of the product so that the customer could see how easy it was to use.

業務員進行產品示範，好讓顧客了解它有多好用。

This handbag comes in many colors.

這款手提包有多種顏色。

新品發表會實用句  PLAY ALL

基本問候

We'd like to thank you for coming to the launch of Heinneman's latest range of software solutions.

我們要感謝各位蒞臨海因門公司最新系列之軟體解決方案的發表會。

I'm really excited to present **our new range of sportswear**.

我真的很高興要介紹我們的新系列運動服。

新品介紹

The 16-megapixel camera is one of the smartphone's **key features**.

一千六百萬畫素相機是這款智慧型手機的主要特色之一。

Office workers, in particular, will love **our new open-source software**.

上班族尤其會喜愛我們的開放原始碼軟體。

Particularly impressive is the ePhone's voice-activation function.

特別讓人印象深刻的是這款電子話機的語音啟動功能。

The new **Zeelex plasma monitor's innovative** features include **touch-screen capabilities and web-based functions**.

此新款 Zeelex 電漿螢幕的創新特色包括觸控與網路功能。

記者提問

I was wondering what makes your **accessories** different from **those** provided by the average supplier.

我想知道是什麼讓你們的飾品有別於一般供應商所提供的產品。

How will you gain an edge on **your rivals**?

你們將如何在競爭對手中取得優勢？

加分應答

Sasprin greatly surpasses its competitors, especially with respect to its long-lasting effects in combating headaches.

Sasprin 大大超過競爭對手，特別是其對抗頭痛的長期效果。

Our new **multifunctional printer** is considerably more advanced than **what's** currently on the market.

我們新的多功能事務機比目前市面上的機種更先進。

We're certain customers will notice **the difference** in the quality of our services.

我們有把握顧客會注意到我們服務品質的差異。

Our goal is for **Skineeze** to be a must-have for any person looking to keep their skin in good condition.

我們的目標是讓 Skineeze 成為任何想維持良好肌膚狀態者的必需品。

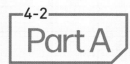

SunBlaster 公司的公關總監葛蘭達（Glenda）與總經理布蘭登（Brendan）在新品發表會上介紹公司的新防曬乳。

G = Glenda   B = Brendan

G: We'd like to thank you for coming to the launch of our new product, SunBlaster. Years of research have **gone into** developing this **remarkable**[1] sunscreen. Let me now introduce our general manager, Brendan Morgan.

B: Thank you, Glenda. I'm really excited to present our new **sensational**[2] sun lotion — SunBlaster! With SunBlaster, we've integrated all the features of a great skin cosmetic without **compromising**[3] on protection. We're sure you'll be as <u>thrilled</u> with SunBlaster as we are!

> 讀做 [θrɪld]，指「極興奮的」，相關用語 thrilled to bits 則指「極開心的」。

我們要感謝各位蒞臨我們新產品 SunBlaster 的發表會。多年的研究讓我們開發出這款效果非凡的防曬乳。現在就讓我介紹我們的總經理布蘭登‧摩根。

謝謝你，葛蘭達。我真的很高興要介紹我們造成轟動的新款防曬乳——SunBlaster！有了 SunBlaster，我們得以整合絕佳肌膚彩妝的所有特色且不讓防護有所妥協。我們有把握你們會跟我們一樣對 SunBlaster 感到興奮無比！

Vocabulary

1. **remarkable** [rɪˋmɑrkəbəl]
adj. 非凡的
The company achieved a remarkable turnaround following months of losses.

2. **sensational** [sɛnˋseʃənl] *adj.* 轟動的
The sensational news story caught the interest of all the people I work with.

G: You're probably wondering what's so special about SunBlaster. Well, particularly impressive are the lotion's moisturizing and soothing <u>properties</u>. Women, **in particular**, will love SunBlaster's **antiaging** effects.

> property [ˋprɑpətɪ] 指「特性；屬性」。

你們可能想知道 SunBlaster 的特別之處。嗯，特別讓人印象深刻的是這款防曬乳的保濕與舒緩特性。女性尤其會喜愛 SunBlaster 的抗老效果。

B: Right. If I may, Glenda, I'd like to discuss our target market more. Women, especially those in the 35 to 55 age **bracket**,[4] will be the main customers. However, we also believe that many men will see the advantages of using SunBlaster.

沒錯。葛蘭達，如果可以的話，我想多討論一下我們的目標市場。女性，特別是 35 至 55 歲的年齡層，將是主要客群。不過，我們也相信許多男性會看見使用 SunBlaster 的優點。

G: Absolutely. Our product can be best summed up by our <u>motto</u>: "SunBlaster: Your skin's best friend."

> 讀做 [ˋmɑto]，指「格言；座右銘」。

的確如此。我們的產品可由我們的格言來完美概括：「SunBlaster，肌膚最好的朋友。」

---

3. **compromise** [ˋkɑmprəˏmaɪz]
   v. 妥協；讓步
   I see we don't agree on this issue, but we will need to compromise.

4. **bracket** [ˋbrækət] n. 等級；類別
   Our campaign is aimed at the 18-30 age bracket.

4-2
Part B　提問與回答

葛蘭達與布蘭登接著開放記者提問。

G = Glenda　R1 = Reporter 1　R2 = Reporter 2　B = Brendan

G: At this point, we'd like to open the press conference to questions.

> point 指「特定時刻」，at this point 即指「現在；此刻」。

現在，我們開放記者會的問答。

R1: Hi, I'm Stuart Chen from the Pineapple Daily. I was wondering what makes your product different from other sunscreens on the market.

嗨，我是鳳梨日報的史都華·陳。我想知道是什麼讓你們的產品有別於市面上的其他防曬乳。

G: Good question, Stuart. SunBlaster is **a cut above** its competitors, especially in terms of ingredients and laboratory testing. We're certain customers will **notice**[1] the difference in quality.

好問題，史都華。SunBlaster 比其競爭者高了一個檔次，尤其是成分與實驗測試的部分。我們有把握顧客會注意到品質上的差異。

Vocabulary

1. **notice** [ˋnotəs] v. 注意；察覺
   I just noticed a new Mexican restaurant has opened down the street.

2. **gain** [gen] v. 獲得
   If you take this job, you'll gain lots of experience.

142

R2: Helen Lu from ABCD TV. How will you **gain**[2] an **edge**[3] on those competitors'?

我是 ABCD 電視台的海倫·盧。你們將如何在競爭對手中取得優勢？

G: The first step will be our unique marketing and ad campaigns. Any more questions?

第一步將是我們獨特的行銷和廣告活動。還有什麼問題嗎？

R1: What promotional channels are you considering?

你們會考慮什麼樣的宣傳管道？

口語用法，指「相關的所有事物」。

G: <u>The works</u> — TV, Internet, and traditional media. Yes, Helen?

所有相關媒介——電視、網路和傳統媒體。是的，海倫？

R2: When will your product **hit the shelves**?

你們的產品何時會上架？

G: The official launch is set for June 10. Stuart, again?

正式上市預定為六月十日。史都華，還有問題嗎？

R1: What will SunBlaster **retail**[4] for?

SunBlaster 的零售價是多少？

B: That's another one of our advantages. At $14.95, the price will be very competitive. If you have any further questions, please contact Glenda. Her phone number and e-mail address are on the press release. Thank you all very much for coming today.

那是我們另一個優勢所在。14.95 美元的價位將非常具競爭性。如果你們有任何進一步的問題，請聯絡葛蘭達。她的電話和電子郵件地址都在新聞稿裡。非常感謝各位今天的蒞臨。

---

3. **edge** [ɛdʒ] *n.* 優勢
   Alistair's family connections gave him an edge when he was looking for his first job.

4. **retail** [ˈriˌtel] *v.* 零售（＋for）
   The new laptop is retailing for much cheaper than similar products on the market.

重點筆記

1. *go into* 投注於……

說明	go into 在英文中的常見用法有：

Ⓐ（時間、金錢等）投注於……（對話用法）

- Many hours went into preparing the feast for the king and queen.
  準備國王與皇后的餐宴耗費多時。

Ⓑ 開始從事（工作、活動等）

- After college, I decided to go into business with a friend of mine.
  大學畢業後，我決定和我的一個朋友一起從商。

Ⓒ 討論；仔細研究

- The doctor talked about the new medicine, but he never went into all of the science behind it.
  醫生談到這款新藥，但他卻從未討論其所有的科學理論。

2. *in particular* 特別是

說明	in particular 為轉折副詞片語，可放在欲強調的動詞片語、名詞或句子後做加強語氣用。同義詞有 especially、particularly、specifically。

- I like studying old languages. In particular, I find ancient Greek fascinating.
  我喜歡研究古老的語言。特別的是，我發現古希臘文十分有趣。

- Most of the paintings in the museum were pretty, but one in particular was a true masterpiece.
  該博物館裡大部分的畫都很美，但有一幅尤其是傑作。

3. *anti-* 反（對）；阻；防（止）

說明	字首 anti- 具「反、抗、防」等含意，多接另一詞構成反義字，常見應用如下： anti- + { aging 老化 = antiaging 抗老的 crime 犯罪 = anticrime 防犯罪的 war 戰爭 = antiwar 反戰的

- Many fruits are thought to have antiaging effects.
  許多水果被認為具抗老效果。

- Antiwar activists continue to protest about the invasion of Iraq.
  反戰激進份子持續對入侵伊拉克表達抗議。

4. *a cut above* 略勝一籌

說明	字面義是「在上方的一記刻痕」，原指比較高而刻下的記號，後比喻為「優於；勝過一籌」。**above** 為形容詞時，**a cut above** 當名詞片語，表示「較優秀的人事物」；**above** 為介系詞時，後面則可加上所勝過的對象。

- We feel our goods are a cut above what is on offer elsewhere.
  我們覺得自家貨品比他處所提供的略勝一籌。

5. *hit the shelves* 上市

說明	此用法以「放到架上」的字面義引申指「上市；上架」，注意 **shelves** 恆為複數形。

- When is that new computer game hitting the shelves?
  那款新的電腦遊戲何時上市？

延伸學習

新品發表會邀請函

新品記者會主旨

Dear Members of the Press:

ZimTek Corp. is pleased to invite you to a press conference to announce the launch of our new tablet PC — bizPad.

舉辦地點與時間

The press conference will be held at the Monarch Hotel at 108 South Ashland Drive at 3 p.m. on Friday, August 14, 2020. Light refreshments will be served following the press conference.

現場提供物品

ZimTek Corp. team members will be on hand at the press conference to answer all your questions. In addition, our tablet PCs will be available for trial use, and press kits will be distributed to every attendee.

出席人數確認

Kindly e-mail your RSVP by July 15 for up to two members of your organization. We look forward to seeing you soon.

Sincerely,

Bradley Hansen
Marketing Manager
ZimTek Corp.
RSVP by sending an e-mail to: events@zimtek.com

中譯

親愛的媒體朋友們：

辛姆塔克公司很高興邀請您參加我們發表新款平板個人電腦 bizPad 的記者會。

這場記者會將於 2020 年 8 月 14 日星期五下午三點假南艾許蘭大道 108 號的尊爵飯店舉辦。記者會後將提供茶點。

辛姆塔克公司全體同仁將在記者會現場回答您所有的問題。此外，我們的平板個人電腦將開放試用，而新聞資料袋也將發給每位出席者。

懇請於 7 月 15 日前回覆，貴機構可出席人數至多為兩人。我們期盼著您的到來。

謹啟

布萊德利‧韓森
行銷經理
辛姆塔克公司
敬請回覆電子郵件至：events@zimtek.com

你 知 道 嗎 ？

press kit「新聞資料袋」是發給媒體的宣傳資料，多用於記者會、新品發表會等場合，常包含以下內容：

- press release 新聞稿
- photos and images 照片和圖像
- media contact information 媒體聯絡資訊
- collateral advertising material 附加的廣告素材
- company background information 公司背景資訊
- fact sheet listing specific features or statistics
  具體特點或數據的實際資料

Talking Your Product Up
介紹產品特色

產品介紹必備句型 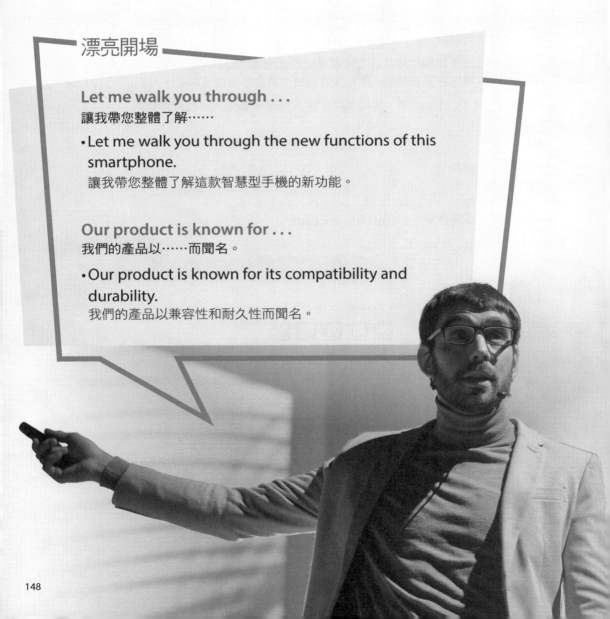 PLAY ALL

漂亮開場

Let me walk you through . . .
讓我帶您整體了解……

- Let me walk you through the new functions of this smartphone.
  讓我帶您整體了解這款智慧型手機的新功能。

Our product is known for . . .
我們的產品以……而聞名。

- Our product is known for its compatibility and durability.
  我們的產品以兼容性和耐久性而聞名。

產品特色

A feature of this product is . . .
這個產品的特色是……

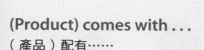

- A feature of this product is its amazing 10 megapixel front-facing camera.
  這個產品的特色是它令人驚艷的一千萬畫素前置相機。

(Product) comes with . . .
（產品）配有……

- This desktop computer comes with a keyboard, mouse, and webcam.
  這台桌上型電腦配有鍵盤、滑鼠與網路攝影機。

This addition has been demonstrated to . . .
此新功能已證明能……

- This addition has been demonstrated to extend the device's battery life.
  此新功能已證明能延長該裝置的電池壽命。

競爭優勢

Allow me to suggest . . .
容我告訴您……

- Allow me to suggest that we lower the price for the first six months after release.
  容我告訴您，這是產品上市半年來，我們首次調降價格。

We carry a large selection of . . .
我們有各式各樣的……

- We carry a large selection of house wares, from end tables to frying pans.
  我們有各式各樣的家庭用品，從茶几到煎鍋都有。

While . . . is our best selling feature, we also have . . .
儘管……是我們的最大賣點，但我們也有……

- While the quality of our goods is our best selling feature, we also have better prices than anyone else in the industry.
  儘管貨物品質是我們的最大賣點，但我們也有比業界任何一家廠商更優惠的價格。

Part A 說明產品優勢

PLAY ALL • TRACK 30

馬克（Mark）向卡爾（Carl）介紹他們新出產的小筆電，並期望卡爾能在其店內販售⋯⋯

M = Mark　　C = Carl

M： Thanks for agreeing to meet with me today, Carl.

卡爾，謝謝你同意今天和我會面。

C： No problem, Mark. What's on your mind?

不客氣，馬克。你有什麼想法呢？

於此指「出售⋯⋯；（商店）備有（貨品）」。

M： So, right now you <u>carry</u> our Inspire laptop in your stores. I'd like to talk to you about stocking our new Inspire Lite netbook as well.

嗯，現在你在店內販售我們的 Inspire 筆電。我想跟你談談是否也能進我們新的 Inspire Lite 小筆電。

C： That's something I might consider. Can you tell me about some of its features?

那可能是我會考慮的事。你能告訴我它的一些特色嗎？

Vocabulary

1. **boast** [bost] *v.* 擁有（值得自豪的東西）
   Germany boasts some of the best beer in the world.

2. **layover** [ˈleˌovə] *n.* 短暫停留
   The businessman was unhappy that his layover in New York was going to be longer than expected.

3. **high-end** [ˈhaɪ ˈɛnd] *adj.* 高階的
   Anthony just bought a high-end laptop for work.

4. **top-of-the-line** [ˈtɑpəvˌðəˈlaɪn] *adj.* （產品）頂級的
   Robin bought a top-of-the-line coffeemaker at the mall today.

M：Of course! First, it's smaller and lighter than any laptop, so the Inspire Lite is perfect for on-the-go businesspeople. And unlike other netbooks with tiny screens, the Inspire Lite **boasts**[1] a huge 13" one.

當然！首先，它比任何筆電都小且輕穎，所以 Inspire Lite 非常適合四處奔波的商務人士。且不像其他小螢幕的小筆電，Inspire Lite 擁有十三吋大的螢幕。

C：Wow, the screen looks great.

哇，螢幕看起來很棒。

M：It's got an HD webcam for conference calls and a 10-hour battery for **layovers**[2] when you need to get a lot of work done.

它有高畫質網路攝影機可供電話會議使用，還有一個供電長達十小時的電池，當你出差在外需要完成大量工作時可使用。

C：What about the hardware?

那硬體方面呢？

M：The Inspire Lite has a **high-end**[3] GPU* that makes graphics really pop and a **top-of-the-line**[4] quad-core* processor.* It's the fastest netbook available today.

Inspire Lite 有高階的圖形處理器，能讓圖像栩栩如生，還有頂級的四核心處理器。這是目前市面上速度最快的小筆電。

C：The device surely must cost a lot since it has so many extra features, right?

這款筆電有這麼多額外的特色，肯定要價不菲，對吧？

M：Nope. We've **outsourced**[5] the hardware so we can pass the savings on to you. It's really very <u>affordable</u>.

不。我們外包硬體的製作，所以可將省下的錢轉給你。這款小筆電真的物美價廉。

讀做 [əˋfɔrdəbəl]，指「付得起的；買得起的」。

---

5. **outsource** [ˋautˏsɔrs] v. 外包
Our company outsourced the production of all components to China.

電腦小詞典

* **GPU**
  n. 圖形處理器（為 graphic processing unit 的簡寫）

* **quad-core** [ˋkwɑdˏkɔr] adj. 四核心的

* **processor** [ˋprɑˏsɛsɚ] n. 處理器

 PLAY ALL • TRACK 31

馬克向卡爾說明公司能提供給經銷商的優惠與銷售方案⋯⋯

C = Carl   M = Mark

C: Well, Mark. You say this device is cheaper than I'd expect. What's the price?

M: It's only $150 per unit. And there are even more features that I haven't told you about.

C: Don't let me stop you.

> carry 於此指「附有；包含」。

M: We are so proud of the specially constructed LCD screen that it carries a lifetime guarantee. It will never break, but if it does, we'll replace it **free of charge**.

嗯，馬克。你說這款小筆電比我預期的還便宜。價格是多少呢？

一台只要一百五十美元。甚至還有更多特色是我還沒跟你說的。

別讓我打斷你。

我們很自豪這款特製的液晶螢幕附有終身保證。它絕不會壞，但如果壞了，我們會免費更換。

Vocabulary

1. **replacement** [rɪ`plesmənt]
   n. 替代（品）
   When the rented motor scooter broke down, Paul asked for a replacement.

2. **reimburse** [ˌriəm`bɝs] *v.* 補償；付還
   My company always reimburses my travel expenses.

C: Free **replacement**?[1] At **point of purchase** or with the manufacturer?

免費更換嗎？在購買處或是向製造商更換？

M: Either one. We'll fully **reimburse**[2] you for any replacement costs you may **incur**.[3] Or the consumer can mail it to our head office, and we'll cover the shipping.

都可以。我們會全額補償你那邊可能產生的更換成本。或是消費者可將小筆電寄送至總公司，我們將負擔運費。

C: What about a hardware warranty?

那硬體的保固呢？

M: We are offering a two-year warranty on hardware and a five-year guarantee on all software bought at the original point of sale.

我們提供兩年的硬體保固，還有在原銷售點所購全數軟體的五年保證。

C: Those are pretty generous terms for the consumer. **What's in it for me?**

那些對消費者來說，是很不錯的條件。對我來說，有什麼好處呢？

指「照成本價格」。

M: If you make an order of 100 units, I'll give you the first 10 <u>at cost</u>. We're sure these netbooks are going to take off **like gangbusters**, and you'll be ordering even more than that soon.

如果你訂購一百台，前十台我會給你成本價。我們確信這些小筆電一定會熱賣，而且你很快就會再訂購比那還要多的數量了。

讀做 [prəˋkjʊrmənt]，指「採購；獲得」。

C: Let me **talk** it **over** with my <u>procurement</u> assistant and get back to you.

讓我跟我的採購助理討論一下，然後再回覆你。

M: OK, but don't wait too long, Carl.

好的。不過，卡爾，可別等太久喔。

---

3. **incur** [ɪnˋkɝ] v. 引起；招致
George incurred late charges when he returned the videos a week after they were due.

153

重點筆記

1. *on-the-go* 四處奔波的

說明	源自 on the go 這個片語，go 為名詞，表示「進行（某事、任務）；開始（活動）」，on the go 遂指「非常忙碌；忙個不停」。對話中則加上連字號成為複合形容詞 on-the-go「四處奔波的」。此外，on the go 也可指某人「積極進取的；有衝勁的」。

- This app is perfect for keeping up with the news if you're someone who's constantly on the go.
  如果你常常很忙，這款應用程式非常適合用來跟上時事。

- Ever since Glen started his own business, he has been constantly on the go.
  自從格倫創業之後，他就一直衝勁十足。

2. *free of charge* 免費地

說明	free of sth 指「免除……」，charge 於此為名詞，指「費用」。free of charge 與 at no cost 意思相同。

- The bikes at this hotel may be used free of charge.
  這間飯店的腳踏車可免費使用。

- Coffee and snacks are provided in the lobby lounge at no cost for all guests.
  咖啡與點心在迎賓大廳免費供應給所有賓客。

3. *point of purchase* 購買處

說明	以「購買點」的字面義形容購買商品的「商店」或「賣場」。

- The coupon is only valid at point of purchase; you cannot contact the supplier for a refund.
  此優惠券只能在購買處使用，你不能聯絡供應商以換取退費。

4. *What's in it for one?* 對某人來說有什麼好處？

說明	為常見的口語用法，表示「某人能從中獲得什麼？」或「這對某人有什麼好處？」。

- I just don't understand why the company would approve the acquisition deal. What's in it for them?
  我就是不理解為何這間公司會批准此收購案。這對他們來說有什麼好處嗎？

5. *like gangbusters* 熱銷；狂賣

說明	gangbuster [ˈgæŋˌbʌstə] 原指「掃蕩黑幫的執法者」，常用 like gangbusters 比喻「威力強大；勢如破竹」或「行動迅速敏捷」。口語中則常用來表示某商品「十分暢銷、熱賣」，也可說成 like hotcakes。jump off the shelves 也有類似含意。

- In the U.S., sports utility vehicles are selling like gangbusters.
  休旅車在美國十分暢銷。

- The new, cheap computers sold like hotcakes.
  這款又新又便宜的電腦賣得非常好。

- My brother is a famous writer, and his books jump off the shelves.
  我的哥哥是位名作家，他的書很暢銷。

6. *talk over* 討論

說明	此為可分動詞片語，若遇代名詞如 it、them 等，要寫成 talk it over 或 talk them over。

- We talked over the problem and tried to solve it.
  我們討論那個問題，並試著予以解決。

4-4 A Promotion Plan
產品宣傳計畫

廣告行銷詞彙與實用句 🔊 PLAY ALL

air [εr] *v.* （電視或廣播節目）播出
Mary's favorite sitcom airs on Tuesday nights at nine o'clock.
瑪麗最愛的情境喜劇於每週二晚間九點播出。

campaign [kæm`pen] *n.* 宣傳活動
We need to pursue a more subtle approach in our campaign.
關於我們的宣傳活動，我們得採取更精細的做法。

premiere [prɪ`mɪr] *n.* （電影或電視節目的）首映
All of the actors and actresses who appeared in the film were invited to attend its premiere.
出現在這部電影的所有男女演員都受邀參加首映會。

selling point *n.* 賣點
Super fast delivery is one of the company's selling points.
超快速配送是該公司的賣點之一。

product placement *n.* 產品置入

The effectiveness of product placement depends on the demographic being targeted and the media form being used to reach them.

產品置入的效益取決於目標族群，以及為了觸及他們所使用的媒體形式。

spokesperson [ˈspoksˌpɝsn̩] *n.* 代言人

A famous golf player became the spokesperson for a large car company.

一位有名的高球選手成為一家大型汽車公司的代言人。

slogan [ˈsloɡən] *n.* 簡短醒目的廣告語

The company's slogan has remained the same since the 1950s.

該公司的廣告標語自 1950 年代起就維持不變。

prime time *n.* 黃金時段

The show first aired during prime time, but it didn't get enough viewers to stay there.

該節目在黃金時段首播，但並沒有吸引足夠的忠實觀眾。

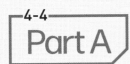

Part A 說明廣宣企畫

奧莉薇（Olive）向席拉（Sheila）和彼得（Peter）報告新產品的宣傳企畫……

O = Olive   S = Sheila   P = Peter

O: Greetings, everyone. Please take a seat. If you don't mind, I'll jump right into my promotion proposal.

大家好。請坐。你們不介意的話，我就直接開始報告我的宣傳企畫了。

S: **We're all ears**, Olive.

奧莉薇，我們洗耳恭聽。

O: Our new acne cleanser will be targeted directly at teenagers. **With that in mind**, we've **nabbed**[1] the female lead from the Thursday night prime-time teen <u>dramedy</u> as our spokesperson.

我們新的痘痘洗面乳將直接鎖定青少年。以此為前提，我們找了週四晚間黃金時段青少年劇情喜劇的女主角來當代言人。

讀做 [ˋdrɑmədi]，指「融合幽默與嚴肅成分的電視劇或電影」。

Vocabulary

1. **nab** [næb] *v.* 取獲；抓住
   Carla was hoping to nab one of the doughnuts before they were all eaten.

2. **reinforce** [͵riənˋfɔrs] *v.* 強化
   The president reinforced his ideas by repeating them several times.

The slogan will be "Fair and Fine." With her perfect complexion* and huge popularity amongst teens, we can't lose.

Plus, we'll have product placement in the show's season opener and at least one other episode.

P: When will the first commercial air?

O: It will premiere in a commercial break during the show's first episode. But wait, there's more.

We've decided to **do away with** pop-up Internet ads and utilize banner ads instead. They're more expensive, but well worth it. They'll **reinforce**[2] brand recognition.

指「品牌辨識度」，即某個品牌能被消費者辨認的程度。

S: Any print ads planned?

O: Just 50 billboards around town at major intersections to get people's attention. They'll **sport**[3] our slogan and promote the "Fair and Fine" lifestyle.

We'll also run radio advertisements on the top two satellite* stations with programming that targets teens.

標語會是「白皙純淨」。有了她完美的膚色以及挾著青少年族群的超高人氣，我們不可能失敗的。

此外，我們將在節目本季首播以及至少另外一集的節目中進行產品置入。

第一支廣告何時會播出？

會在節目首集的廣告時段中首播。但等等，還不只這樣。

我們已決定取消彈出式網路廣告，改採橫幅式廣告。那比較貴，但會非常值得的。它們能強化品牌辨識度。

有任何平面廣告的計畫嗎？

只有城區主要路口的五十個大型廣告看板以吸引民眾的注意。上面會主打我們的廣告標語並宣傳「白皙純淨」的生活方式。

我們也會在最紅的兩個衛星電台當中，以青少年為主要族群的節目裡播放廣告。

---

3. **sport** [spɔrt] v. 炫耀；誇示
Bob is sporting his new Gucci shoes.

字彙補給站

＊ **complexion** [kəmˋplɛkʃən] n. 膚色

＊ **satellite** [ˋsætəˌlaɪt] n. 人造衛星

4-4
Part B 說明廣宣細節

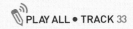 PLAY ALL • TRACK 33

奧麗薇播放宣傳廣告並向大家進行
相關說明……

O = Olive   P = Peter   S = Sheila

O: I trust everyone had a nice lunch break? Good. Then I'll get right back to my plan.

P: We've heard a lot about the ads, Olive, but what exactly will they look like?

O: Take a look. Ads will feature an all-white background with shades of blue. Our leading lady will be dressed in an all-white ensemble* as she splashes her face with water.

我相信大家都有個愉快的午休時間吧？好的。那麼我們就直接回到我的計畫吧。

奧莉薇，我們聽了很多關於廣告方面的資訊，但實際呈現的樣子會如何呢？

請看。廣告主要會是全白的基底搭配藍色調。我們的女主角將穿著全白的整套服裝，同時會以清水潑打她的臉龐。

Vocabulary

1. **striking** [ˋstraɪkɪŋ]
   adj. 醒目的；很有魅力的
   The woman on stage looked striking in her bright yellow dress.

2. **eye-catching** [ˋaɪˏkætʃɪŋ]
   adj. 引人注目的
   Brenda used eye-catching graphics in her presentation.

The billboards will also feature a lot of white, with a few bright colors. White is **striking**[1] and **eye-catching**[2] and subliminally* suggests that a clear complexion can be achieved when you use our product.

廣告看板也會以大量白色為主，加上一些明亮的色彩。白色醒目亦吸引目光，且下意識地讓人感覺，使用我們的產品時，就能擁有潔淨膚色。

S: You want teens to **covet**[3] her perfect complexion and the perfect life it implies?

你想要青少年渴望擁有廣告所傳達的如女主角般的完美膚色和美好生活？

O: Exactly. We'll highlight our product's ability to clear up acne-prone skin while showing off how much our star enjoys using it. Those are some great selling points!

沒錯。我們將標榜我們的產品能清潔痘痘肌，同時展現我們的明星多喜歡使用這項產品。那些都是很棒的賣點！

P: I get the feeling you've **put a lot of thought into** this campaign, Olive.

奧莉薇，我感覺你在這個宣傳活動上花了很多的心思。

O: Thank you. I've spent a lot of time getting it all planned out. Lastly, we'll send out direct mailers to 2,500 suburban households that include a 50-percent off coupon two weeks before the commercials air. We're set to **make a bundle**!

謝謝你。我花了很多時間來完成所有計畫。最後，廣告播出前的兩個星期，我們會寄送廣告傳單至郊區的兩千五百戶家庭，裡面有五折的折價券。我們準備好要大賺一筆了！

S: Great!

太好了！

P: Good work!

做得好！

O: Thanks. Your approval means a lot.

謝謝。你們的肯定對我來說意義重大。

---

3. **covet** [ˈkʌvət] v. 垂涎；渴望
   If the public didn't covet what the stars wore, the fashion industry would be very different.

字彙補給站

* **ensemble** [ɑnˈsɑmbəl] n. 整套服裝

* **subliminally** [səˈblɪmənəli] adv. 下意識地

重點筆記

1. *be all ears* 洗耳恭聽

說明	誇飾地形容聽話的一方彷彿身上長滿了耳朵，引申指「洗耳恭聽；仔細聆聽」。另外，**be all eyes** 指「全神貫注地看著」。

- I'd love to hear some suggestions for fixing our shipping problems. I'm all ears.
  我很樂意聽聽能解決我們出貨問題的一些建議。我洗耳恭聽。

- Everyone in the audience was all eyes as the presenter revealed the prototype.
  主持人揭曉產品原型時，每個觀眾都全神貫注地看著。

2. *with sth in mind* 有……的想法

說明	with sth in mind 指「把……記在心裡；有……的想法」，對話中的 **with that in mind** 可表示「有鑑於此；這樣看來」，**that** 用來指稱先前所提過的某件事。

- There won't be another bus for an hour. With that in mind, we should find a cool place to wait.
  一個小時內不會有公車。這樣看來，我們應該找個涼爽的地方等待。

3. *do away with* 廢除；除去；擺脫

說明	此動詞片語代表「廢止；除去；擺脫」，與 **get rid of** 意義相同。此語亦可指「殺掉……」，為口語用法。

- Legislators did away with the unpopular law.
  立法人員廢止了這條不受歡迎的法令。

- There were rumors that the landlord had done away with his wife.
  有謠言指出房東殺了他太太。

4. *acne-prone* 易長痘痘的

說明	字根 -prone 表示「有……傾向的；很可能的」，前面多接名詞構成複合形容詞，表示「易有某項特質的」，常見應用如下： acne +　　　　　　　　　= acne-prone　易長痘痘的 accident +　} + -prone　= accident-prone　易出事故的 injury +　　　　　　　　= injury-prone　易受傷的

- Alan is an athlete who is injury-prone.
  艾倫是個很容易受傷的運動員。

5. *put a lot of thought into* 花很多心力在……

說明	以字面義「投注很多想法」比喻「花很多心力去做某件事」。

- Carol always puts a lot of thought into the gifts she gives her friends.
  卡蘿總是花很多心力在準備給朋友的禮物上。

6. *make a bundle* 賺大錢；收入豐厚

說明	make a bundle 與 make a pile 都可指「賺大錢」，bundle 與 pile 分別比喻賺了「大捆」及「大疊」的鈔票。

- Ryan made a bundle on the stock market and retired early.
  萊恩在股市中賺了一大筆錢，很早就退休了。

產品促銷計畫好用句 🔊 PLAY ALL

**商討
促銷模式**

We've put together (type) bundle of (products).

我們將（產品）搭成（類別）的銷售組合。

- We've put together a four-bottle bundle of our skin-care products.

  我們將公司的護膚產品搭成四瓶的銷售組合。

We've got (number) winning ideas for . . .

針對……，我們已有（數目）個必勝的點子。

- We've got five winning ideas for our social media campaign.

  針對我們的社群媒體活動，我們已有五個必勝的點子。

Our brand is teaming up with . . .

我們的品牌正與……合作。

- Our brand is teaming up with several online celebrities to get our product in front of people.

  我們的品牌正與幾個網紅合作，
  要把產品呈現在大眾面前。

**制定
促銷折扣**

Customers will receive (percent) discount on (products).

顧客購買（產品）將享有（百分比）的折扣。

• Customers will receive a 20 percent discount on the software products.

顧客購買軟體產品將享有八折的折扣。

Customers will get (percent) off (products).

顧客將享有（產品）（幾折）的優惠。

• Customers will get 15 percent off all our products.

顧客將享有全數商品八五折的優惠。

At participating stores, we'll be offering (percent) off (products) and . . .

在配合的店家內，我們將提供（產品）（幾折）的優惠，以及……

• At participating stores, we'll be offering 10 percent off individual lipsticks and a NT$50 coupon.

在配合的店家內，我們將提供單支口紅九折的優惠，以及一張五十元的折價券。

**定位
促銷族群**

Since our (products) are targeted at (group), we're really trying to . . .

由於我們的（產品）是以（群體）為目標族群，我們真的試著……

• Since our cereals are targeted at families, we're really trying to emphasize the fresh ingredients and the convenience angles.

由於我們的麥片是以家庭為目標族群，我們真的試著強調新鮮食材以及便利的角度。

The special set will be sold to (type of demographic).

這個特惠組合將以（特定族群）為銷售對象。

• The special set will be sold to stay-at-home dads.

這個特惠組合將以全職爸爸為銷售對象。

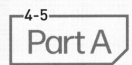

Part A 說明行銷通路

PLAY ALL • TRACK 34

席拉（Sheila）和班（Ben）向阿方索（Alfonso）報告公司產品在假期季節的通路行銷方案。

A = Alfonso   S = Sheila   B = Ben

A: Let's talk promotions. How's the big holiday **push**[1] **coming along**?

我們來討論促銷吧。假期大促銷活動進展得如何了？

S: To start, we've put together a 10-pack bundle of all our flavored instant noodles. The special set will be sold online and at hypermarkets.

首先，我們將所有口味的即食麵搭成十包的銷售組合。這個特惠組合將在網路和量販店販售。

A: The packaging is very eye-catching and will certainly **stand out** in <u>big-box stores</u> and on visually crowded e-commerce sites. Tell me about the deals.

包裝非常吸睛，在超級大賣場和令人眼花撩亂的電商網站上勢必會格外顯眼。跟我說説販售的內容吧。

big-box store 指「超級大賣場」，類似説法有 megastore、supercenter、superstore。

Vocabulary

1. **push** [pʊʃ]
n.（做生意為贏得優勢而進行的）努力
This month, we are making a big advertising push to promote the line.

2. **cover** [ˋkʌvə] *v.* 負擔
Our manufacturers are raising prices to cover the cost of materials.

S: At hypermarkets, customers will receive a 15 percent discount on the bundle. They'll also be entered into a <u>raffle</u> to win two free tickets to Jungle Land on purchases over NT$2,000.

在量販店，顧客將享有八五折的組合價。消費超過新台幣兩千元，他們也能參加抽獎活動，可贏得兩張森林樂園的免費門票。

讀做 [ˈræfəl]，指「抽獎」。

B: Online customers will get 20 percent off all our products, and for orders over NT$1,000, we'll **cover**[2] shipping.

線上顧客將享有全數商品八折的優惠，而超過一千元的訂單，我們會負擔運費。

A: Smart, **given the fact that** many consumers do their holiday shopping exclusively online nowadays. What about grocery stores?

聰明，這考量到許多消費者如今只在線上進行假期購物。那食品雜貨店呢？

grocer [ˈɡrosə] 指「食品雜貨店」。

S: At **participating**[3] <u>grocers</u>, we'll be offering 10 percent off individual packages and a NT$50 coupon.

在配合的食品雜貨店內，我們將提供單包九折的優惠，以及一張五十元的折價券。

A: Why not just do a two-for-one deal?

為什麼不做買一送一的活動呢？

B: We want to **encourage**[4] holiday buyers to become repeat shoppers.

我們想鼓勵假期購買者成為回購顧客。

---

3. **participating** [pɑrˈtɪsəˌpetɪŋ] *adj.* 配合的；參與的

Participating employees will receive the day off to attend the course.

4. **encourage** [ɪnˈkɜɪdʒ] *v.* 鼓勵

We encourage our employees to share their ideas openly with management.

Part B 說明宣傳活動

席拉和班接著報告他們打算在社群媒體上進行的宣傳活動。

A = Alfonso   B = Ben   S = Sheila

A: Are we doing anything on Instagram or Facebook?

我們要在 Instagram 或臉書上進行任何活動嗎？

B: We've actually got three winning ideas for our social media blitz.

針對社群媒體的密集宣傳，我們其實已有三個必勝的點子。

S: In one competition, families can post photos of themselves enjoying our noodles with the hashtag "rainbownoodles."

在其中一個比賽當中，各個家庭可貼出他們享用即食麵的照片，上頭標註了「彩虹麵條」。

Vocabulary

1. **customize** [ˋkʌstəˏmaɪz]
   v. 客製化；訂做

   Shoppers can customize their sneakers online by choosing from different designs and colors.

2. **award** [əˋwɔrd] v. 頒給

   The best salesperson this month will be awarded a $400 bonus.

A: Great idea! It totally breaks the stereotype* that instant noodles are eaten alone. What else have you got?

很棒的主意！這完全打破即食麵只能獨自享用的刻板印象。你們還有什麼想法？

B: Our patrons are always **customizing**[1] their ramen, so we'll also be seeking submissions* of their most <u>wild- and out-there</u> culinary* creations under the same hashtag.

我們的顧客總會客製化自己的麵食，所以我們也將尋求他們在相同的標註下，交出最瘋狂且特別的烹飪創作。

> wild- and out-there 為複合形容詞，屬誇飾用法，指「瘋狂且不尋常的」。

A: Got ya. What is this about mukbangs?

了解。關於吃播的內容是什麼？

S: Mukbang videos are a perfect medium for showing how delicious our noodles are.

吃播影片是展現我們的麵有多好吃的絕佳媒介。

B: Those clips* **never fail to** give me an appetite.

那些短片總能讓我胃口大開。

A: Me too, **come to think of it**. Are we offering any prizes?

這樣一想，我也是。我們有提供任何獎品嗎？

B: Yes. The company will **award**[2] the winner of each category two round-trip tickets to Japan based on the popularity and uniqueness of their photo or video.

有的。根據其照片或影片的受歡迎度與獨特性，公司將頒發各兩張日本來回機票給每個項目的優勝者。

S: Having such great prizes should help us **entice**[3] posts and **drum up** buzz.

有這麼棒的獎品應該能幫助我們吸引貼文並激起話題了。

---

3. **entice** [ɪnˋtaɪs] v. 吸引；引誘
   To entice consumers into the store, we held a huge sale on opening day.

字彙補給站

* **stereotype** [ˋstɛrɪəˌtaɪp] n. 刻板印象
* **submission** [səbˋmɪʃən] n. 提交
* **culinary** [ˋkʌləˌnɛri] adj. 烹飪的
* **clip** [klɪp] n. 短片

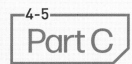
Part C　說明代言計畫

最後，班報告名人代言與實體活動
的行銷計畫。

B = Ben　　S = Sheila　　A = Alfonso

B: Since our noodles are **targeted**[1] at families, we're really trying to **play up** the fresh ingredients and the convenience angles.

由於我們的麵食是以家庭為目標族群，我們真的試著強調新鮮食材和便利的角度。

指「（為解決某個問題或做某件事情的）必找的」。

S: We want to be the go-to meal for households this holiday season when they need something quick but can't find a place to eat.

這個假期季節，當家家戶戶需要快速解決，卻找不到地方用餐時，我們想成為他們所選擇的餐點。

A: You guys **paint a** pretty **picture**, but how are we going to **make it a reality**?

你們描繪了美麗的願景，但我們要怎麼讓它成真呢？

Vocabulary

1. **target** [ˋtɑrɡɪt] v. 以……為目標
   We mainly target adult women as they make most household purchasing decisions.

2. **savor** [ˋsevɚ] v. 品嚐；品味
   Nicole savored the amazing steak at the fancy bistro.

B: Our brand is **teaming up with** YouTuber and chef Lewis Babbish to get our product in front of people.

> 以字面義「廣泛的吸引力」形容「廣受喜愛」。

A: Great choice. Lewis has <u>broad appeal</u> and can show how easy it is to cook our noodles. What will he be doing?

> livestream [ˈlaɪvˌstrim] 指「透過網路即時播出影音內容」，即「直播」。

B: To start, some <u>livestreams</u> of him unboxing, cooking, and **savoring**[2] each one of our noodle offerings.

A: Like a mukbang.

S: Exactly. We think this will further **drive**[3] traffic to our website and increase brand awareness.

A: Is that all?

S: We've also got some live events lined up with Lewis.

A: Good. If we're lucky, that might **garner**[4] some media attention.

我們的品牌正與 YouTube 網紅暨廚師路易斯・巴畢許合作，要把產品呈現在大眾面前。

選得好。路易斯廣受喜愛，又能展現烹煮我們的麵條有多容易。他要做什麼呢？

首先是直播一些他開箱、烹煮並品嚐我們各類麵條的畫面。

就像吃播一樣。

沒錯。我們認為這會進一步驅動網站流量並提升品牌識別度。

就這些嗎？

我們也已經和路易斯安排了一些現場活動。

很好。如果我們幸運的話，那或許會獲得一些媒體關注。

---

3. **drive** [draɪv] *v.* 驅使
The tech industry has been driving growth in the U.S. economy for many years.

4. **garner** [ˈɡɑrnɚ] *v.* 獲得
Olivia's discovery garnered a lot of praise from the scientific community.

重點筆記

1. *come along* 進展

說明	come along 在英文中的常見用法有：

Ⓐ 進展（對話用法）

Preparations for the event are coming along really well.

這場活動的準備工作進展得很順利。

Ⓑ 跟隨

Dan is coming along with us to join the monthly meeting.

丹跟著我們一起去開月例會議。

Ⓒ 出現

Taylor looked for a new job for months before the right one came along.

直到對的選擇出現之前，泰勒花了好幾個月找新工作。

2. *stand out* 顯眼；突出

說明	此片語形容因為優異而「突出」或「顯眼」，常見應用為 stand out from the crowd「脫穎而出」。

- The laptop's innovative design helped it stand out from similar products.

  此筆電的創新設計使其從類似產品中脫穎而出。

3. *given the fact that* 有鑒於……

說明	given 在此為介系詞，指「考量到……」，given the fact that 亦可簡化為 given that。

- Given the fact that Ian is the most qualified, he'll probably get the promotion.

  有鑒於伊恩是最符合資格的，他可能會獲得升遷。

4. *never fail to* 總是能……

說明	fail [fel] 指「失敗」，never fail to 以雙重否定的形式強調「從未做不到……」，指「總是能……」。

- Elsa never failed to give an outstanding presentation while working as a sales rep here.
  艾莎在這裡當業代時，總能進行相當出色的簡報。

5. *come to think of it* 這樣一想

說明	常用於談及某個話題時，突然想到與之相關聯的人事物。

- The meeting is next Wednesday, which, come to think of it, is also the date of my dentist's appointment.
  會議是下週三，這樣一想，也是我預約看牙醫的日期。

6. *drum up* 激發

說明	drum [drʌm] 當動詞時指「敲擊；敲打」，drum up 則形容「增加對某事物的興趣或支持」。

- The political candidate is holding several events to drum up support from voters.
  這名政治候選人正在舉行幾場活動，要激發選民的支持。

7. *play up* 強調

說明	此片語動詞指「強調」，形容試著說服人們去相信某事物的重要性。

- Melissa played up her internship experience when interviewing for accounting positions.
  梅麗莎在面試會計職缺時強調了她的實習經驗。

8. *paint a(n) . . . picture* 描繪……的願景

說明	以字面義「畫一幅……的畫」引申指「描繪……的願景」，中間常加形容詞來修飾願景的特性。

- **The sales forecasts do not** paint an **optimistic** picture.
  銷售預測顯得不甚樂觀。

9. *make sth a reality* 讓某事成真

說明	reality [rɪˋælətɪ] 指「現實；事實」，make sth a reality 即形容「讓某事成真」。

- **After many years, Dennis** made **his dream of going back to school** a reality.
  多年後，丹尼斯重返校園的夢想成真了。

10. *team up with* 與……聯手、合作

說明	team 原指「隊伍」，team up 則表示「組隊」以一同努力達到某特定目標，即「合作」之意。

- **Sally** teamed up with **Tim to get the project done on time.**
  莎莉與提姆合作好準時完成這個專案。

11. *line up* 安排；準備

說明	line up 的字面義為「排隊」，亦可指「準備；組織；安排」。

- **After the Christmas sale finishes, we have more promotions** lined up **for January.**
  聖誕特賣結束後，我們還準備了更多的一月分促銷活動。

延伸學習

行銷小百科

blitz
[blɪts] 密集宣傳

blitz 原指「閃電攻擊」，用於行銷領域則指「集中火力的宣傳活動」。

mukbang
[ˋmʊkˏbɑŋ] 吃播

此字為韓語「吃飯」和「直播」的組合，為韓國率先興起的一種網路文化。直播主在鏡頭前上演飲食真人秀，藉此與觀眾交流試吃心得。

buzz
[bʌz] 話題

buzz 原指「昆蟲飛行時所發出的低而持續的聲音」，用於行銷則指「話題；轟動」，而 create/make a buzz 即指「創造話題；引發轟動」。

brand awareness
[əˋwɛrnəs] 品牌識別度

指品牌被消費者認識或識別的能力，是關係到消費者購買與否的要素，也是品牌發展策略的關鍵因素。

參展籌備

參展籌備好用句 PLAY ALL

編列預算

A: Twenty booths at this electronics expo are well within our budget.

此電子產品展的二十個攤位非常符合我們的預算。

B: Good. Go ahead and put down a deposit.

很好。就去付訂金吧。

商展地點

A: If we choose the trade show in New York, the travel costs will eat up a huge part of the allocated funds.

如果我們選擇紐約的商展，差旅費將吃掉一大部分的撥款。

B: Still, I think the international exposure would be well worth it.

儘管如此，我認為國際曝光度是值得的。

商展策略

A: How should we handle staff training so they are confident when speaking about the new product?

我們該如何進行人員訓練，才能讓他們在談論新產品時信心十足？

B: I'm working on a cheat sheet of product features, and let's set up a training session for next week.

我正在做產品特色的小抄，我們下週辦個訓練課程吧。

旅程安排

A: The convention center has blocked out rooms at an adjoining hotel at group rates.

會議中心細心地以團體價在鄰近的飯店安排房間。

B: Excellent. We'll need three rooms for all five days and please ask about a late checkout.

棒極了。我們這五天需要三個房間，請要求晚一點退房。

Part A 說明籌備進度

亨利（Henry）針對即將來臨的商展與相關同仁討論籌備事宜……

H = Henry　　I = Ian

H: Thanks for coming, everyone. As you all know, it's trade show season. And before we all start **gearing up** for this year's <u>circuit</u>, I just want to go over some things.

讀做 [ˋsɝkət]，指「巡迴；巡遊」。

感謝大家的光臨。大家都知道的，現正值商展時期。而在我們全體開始為今年的展覽做準備之前，我想先說明一些事項。

As usual, we will be renting out a pair of booths at each of the major shows, and representatives from Sales, Distribution, and Customer Service will **man**[1] each one.

一如以往，我們會在每一個主要展覽會場租一組攤位，業務部、經銷部以及客服部的代表將派員負責各場展覽。

I: Excuse me, Henry. Will you be the one assigning **shifts**?[2]

不好意思，亨利。會是你負責安排輪班嗎？

Vocabulary

1. **man** [mæn] *v.* 為……配備人手
Janice offered to man the register while Corey took his break.

2. **shift** [ʃɪft] *n.* 輪班
The shift most employees work is the usual nine to five.

H: No. Each department will be responsible for choosing which employees to send. And everyone that goes should be prepared to be busy.

不會。各部門將負責選擇所派遣的員工。而每一個前往的人都應做好會非常忙碌的準備。

To make our presence more effective this year, we'll be upping the signage budget to attract more visitors. Of course, we had to rearrange some things to **accommodate**[3] this, so the minor shows will be taking a back seat. We will only be attending a select few <u>trade only</u> small ones.

為了讓我們的能見度在今年更具效益，我們將增加招牌的預算以吸引更多的參觀者。當然，我們得因此做些調整，所以小型展覽將會是次要的選擇。我們只會參加特定少數的小型商業型展覽。

指「商業的；商務的」。

I: Sorry, one more question. Why choose the trade only shows over the public ones?

抱歉，我還有個疑問。為何只選擇商業型的展覽而不是公眾型的展覽？

H: There just isn't enough of a **payoff**[4] for the public shows to be worthwhile. Usually, the <u>head counts</u> are quite low, and the people that do come aren't really serious about buying.

參與公眾型展覽的投資報酬率實在不高。通常來客數都很低，而來的客人通常都不是真正的消費者。

head count 指「清點人數；總人數」。

Well, now that I'm done with the overview, how about we take a short break and then meet back here in 15 to finish up?

嗯，既然我已做完摘要報告了，我們先休息一下吧，十五分鐘後再回來做總結。

---

3. **accommodate** [əˋkɑməˌdet]
   v. 適應；順應
   When clients make a request, we do all we can to accommodate them.

4. **payoff** [ˋpeˌɔf] *n.* 收益；回報
   It takes time to develop a successful business, but the payoff can be huge.

Part B 分派工作項目

亨利接著說明展覽的相關工作項目
與人事需求……

H = Henry   C = Claire   I = Ian

H: Are there any questions before I continue? No? All right, let's move on to **delegating**[1] assignments.

First, while I'll be **overseeing**[2] everything, I need somebody to take charge of each individual show. This could be a great opportunity for someone to prove they've got what it takes to handle more responsibility in the future.

I will post a list of show dates in HR, and just put your name by the one you want.

在我繼續之前,有沒有任何疑問?沒有嗎?那好,我們接著來分派職務。

首先,在我監督所有事務的同時,我需要有人負責統籌每一場展覽。這會是個證明個人在未來能擔當更多責任的大好機會。

我會在人資部張貼展覽日期的清單,只要將你的名字填在想負責的日期旁邊就行了。

Vocabulary

1. **delegate** [ˈdɛləˌget] v. 委派
   The manager delegated all his work to his staff.

2. **oversee** [ˌovɚˈsi] v. 監督;管理
   As a supervisor, it is my job to oversee all the work done in my department.

Make sure you sign up by Friday. That's when I'll be making my final decisions about who will be in charge of each show.

C: Henry, is there a limit to how many we can **volunteer**[3] to run?

H: Always an **eager beaver**, Claire! There is no official limit, but I think it would be wise to do no more than one a week.

This will be an extremely busy month, and I don't want anyone to **overburden**[4] themselves to the point that they can't help others when need arises.

指「在幕後；在後台；秘密地」。

Now, for those who would like to help out behind the scenes, I also need two to three people to work directly with Marketing to create ads and signage that will really make us stand out.

I: Do we need a background in graphic design to be considered for that?

H: No. I'll consider anyone who seems creative and wants to work hard. Well, I think that's everything for now.

請務必於星期五前完成報名。屆時我會決定好由誰來負責每一場展覽。

亨利，是否有限制我們能自願負責的場次？

克萊兒，你總是積極又熱心！沒有明文限制，但我認為最好一週不要負責超過一場。

這將會是非常忙碌的一個月，我不希望有人負擔過重到若有需要協助時，他們會無法配合的程度。

嗯，至於那些想在幕後幫忙的人，我也會需要兩到三個同仁直接跟行銷部門合作，設計出能讓我們的攤位更顯眼的廣告和招牌。

我們是否得有美術設計背景才能做為考慮人選？

不用。任何具有想像力且想要努力的人我都會考慮。嗯，我想目前所有的事項都談到了。

---

3. **volunteer** [ˌvɑlənˈtɪr] v. 自願
Charlie volunteered to work at the animal shelter.

4. **overburden** [ˌovəˈbɜdn̩] v. 使負擔過重
Sarah didn't want to overburden her assistants with too much work, but she needed a lot of help.

重點筆記

1. *gear up* 全力準備;蓄勢待發

說明	gear [gɪr] 指「裝備;齒輪」,gear up 原為「將一切所需裝備準備好」之意,gear up for sth 則指「準備好進行某項任務」。

- The company's gearing up for the big export drive.
  該公司正全力準備大規模出口。

2. *take a back seat* 扮演次要的角色

說明	back seat「後座」用來比喻「次要位置」,take a back seat 表示「把領先的位置讓出來」,即「退居幕後;甘願居於他人之下」的意思。

- During the war, all manufacturing had to take a back seat to military needs.
  戰爭時期,所有製造業都必須屈居於軍事需求之下。

3. *a select few* 特定少數

說明	select 指「精選的;最優秀的」,few 指「少數」,a select few 即表示「特定少數」。

- These activities should be available to all citizens, not just a select few.
  這樣的活動應該讓所有市民都能參加,而不只是特定少數。

4. *be done with* 完成……

說明	形容「完成或結束某事物」,類似用法為 bring to completion。

- Let's spend another half an hour discussing the project and then be done with it.
  我們再花半個小時討論這個專案,然後結束吧。

5. *take charge of* 負責；管理

說明	charge 當名詞有「照管；責任」的意思，take charge of 遂指「負責；管理」。

- Who will take charge of the department when Simon leaves?
  賽門離開後，誰將會管理這個部門？

6. *have got what it takes to + V.*
擁有……的能力、特質

說明	take 在此為動詞，指「需要；要求」，have got what it takes to + V. 即形容「擁有做某事所需的能力、特質」。

- Kelly has got what it takes to be a professional musician.
  凱莉擁有擔任職業音樂家的能力。

7. *eager beaver* 勤奮工作者

說明	eager [ˋigɚ] 指「熱心的」，beaver [ˋbivɚ] 指「海狸」，海狸會築巢、搭壩，被視為是一種勤奮的動物。eager beaver 即用來形容「有高度工作熱誠，能承擔重任，也比他人更努力工作的人」。

- Steven is a real eager beaver. He always shows up to work early and offers to help anyone who needs a hand.
  史蒂芬真的很認真工作。他總是很早來上班，還會幫忙任何有需要的人。

延伸學習

參展籌備實用詞彙

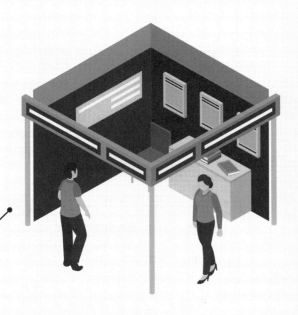

trade fair/show 商展
exhibition [ˌɛksəˈbɪʃən] 展覽

organizer [ˈɔrgəˌnaɪzə] 主辦單位
exhibitor [ɪgˈzɪbətə] 參展商
attendee [əˌtɛnˈdi] 參展民眾
traffic flow 會場流量

booth [buθ] 攤位
floor plan（展場攤位）配置圖
signage [ˈsaɪnɪdʒ] 招牌
product demo 商品展示

分派任務好用句

說明人員需求

- I need the sales department to take charge of this year's trade show.

  我需要業務部來負責今年的商展。

- This task requires someone with an eye for detail and a sense of style.

  這份工作需要觀察細微並有時尚感的人。

尋求自願者

- Who's going to take this assignment? Any volunteers?

  誰要接這項任務？有自願者嗎？

- Does anyone want to take this assignment?

  有人想接這項任務嗎？

指派適合人選

- I think you'd be a great choice for this task.

  我想你會是這項工作的絕佳人選。

- I'd like you to be in charge of this project.

  我希望你來負責這項專案。

UNIT
5

Company Operations
公司運作

Press Conferences
英語記者會

圖解記者會現場 PLAY ALL

Let me start over there.
What is your question?
我們從這裡開始。您的問題是什麼呢？

① **projector** [prə`dʒɛktə] 投影機
② **projector screen** [skrin] 投影屏幕
③ **host** [host] 主持人
④ **podium** [`podiəm] 講台
⑤ **microphone** [`maɪkrə͵fon] 麥克風
⑥ **speaker** [`spikə] 喇叭
⑦ **video camera** [`kæmərə] 攝影機
⑧ **headset** [`hɛd͵sɛt] 耳機
⑨ **camera operator** [`apə͵retə] 錄影師
⑩ **photographer** [fə`tɑgrəfə] 攝影師
⑪ **reporter** [rɪ`pɔrtə] 記者
⑫ **media/press kit** 新聞資料袋

記者會開場說明

PLAY ALL ● TRACK 39

自行車公司的科技長艾倫（Alan）與公關經理派蒂（Patty）召開記者會說明產品回收的緣由。

A = Alan　　P = Patty

A: Good afternoon. Thank you all for **making it** here today. I'm Alan Levinson, <u>chief technology officer</u> for Rapida.

午安。感謝各位今天來到這裡。我是艾倫‧李文森，利必達公司的科技長。

指「科技長」，可簡寫為 CTO。
其他常見的企業職稱有：
· chief executive officer (CEO)　執行長
· chief financial officer (CFO)　財務長
· chief operating officer (COO)　營運長

P: And I'm Patty Fields, <u>PR</u> manager.

而我是公關經理派蒂‧菲爾德斯。

PR 為 public relations「公關」的縮寫。

Vocabulary

1. **arise** [əˋraɪz] v. 產生；出現
Paranoia and infighting began to arise as the boss fired staff one by one.

2. **detail** [ˋditel] v. 詳細描述
The CEO wrote a book detailing his rise from lowly salesman to boss of the company.

A: Before we **get down to business**, we'd like to give a quick outline of today's press conference.

在我們進入正題以前，我們想快速簡介今天的記者會。

> defect [ˈdiˌfɛkt] 指「瑕疵；缺陷」，可接介系詞 in 來指稱有缺陷的事物。

P: As you know, <u>defects</u> in our Trekker 2000 led to our recent <u>recall</u> of the model.

如各位所知，奇航者 2000 的瑕疵導致我們近期召回這款車型。

> 讀做 [rɪˈkɔl]，指「召回」。另有「記憶力；記性」的意思，如 powers of recall「記憶力」。

A: Today, we will be explaining how these issues **arose**[1] and **detailing**[2] the steps we'll be taking to **resolve**[3] them.

今天，我們將解釋這些問題的成因，並詳述我們會採取的解決步驟。

> complaint [kəmˈplent] 指「投訴；不滿」，常搭配 file、make、receive 等動詞。

P: Over the past two weeks, we've received several thousand <u>complaints</u> relating to two main problems. We'll now be **fielding**[4] questions on the specifics.

過去兩週來，我們收到和兩個主要問題相關的數千件客訴。我們將針對這些細節來回答問題。

3. **resolve** [rɪˈzɑlv] *v.* 解決；消除
The two companies' dispute over the product patent proved impossible to resolve.

4. **field** [fild] *v.* 巧妙地答覆
Customer service agents began to field complaints from numerous customers after the defect was publicized.

191

Part B 開放記者提問

PLAY ALL ● TRACK 40

與會記者迪娜（Dina）和雷夫（Ralph）詢問產品出包的原因。

D = Dina　　A = Alan　　R = Ralph　　P = Patty

D: Dina Anderson, Morning Times. You've said one issue is related to chains coming loose on the bikes. That's a pretty serious problem. Could you explain the exact <u>nature</u> of the defect?

讀做 [netʃə]，指「本質；種類」。

迪娜・安德森，早晨時報。你們提到一個問題和鏈條從自行車鬆脫有關。那是個相當嚴重的問題。你們能解釋這個瑕疵究竟是什麼嗎？

A: In a nutshell, it stems from faulty* derailleurs.*

簡單來說，問題出在有缺陷的變速器。

Vocabulary

1. pop out [pɑp] *v.* 突然跳出、彈出
The athlete's shoulder popped out of its socket, but he was still somehow able to finish the game.

2. ascertain [͵æsə`ten] *v.* 查明；弄清
By analyzing customer survey results, the company was able to ascertain which advertisement was most effective.

D: There have also been many <u>cases</u> of the front tire **popping out**[1] of the | rim.* What's happening there?

還有很多前輪輪胎從輪圈脫落的案例。那是怎麼回事？

case 於此指「具體情況；實例」。

A: Yes, we've **ascertained**[2] it's a **structural**[3] problem with the wheel hubs.* Yes, over there, please.

是的，我們已查明是和輪軸有關的結構性問題。好的，那邊那位請說。

R: Ralph Bellamy, News Source International. These are fairly basic design faults. How did something like this **slip through the** quality control **net**?

雷夫‧貝勒米，國際新聞來源報。這些都是相當基本的設計缺失。這類情況怎麼會在品管網絡中漏掉呢？

讀做 [ˈfæsət]，指「（問題、形勢等的）方面」。

P: It's basically a <u>facet</u> of the new lightweight technology we developed for this model. Naturally, we're disappointed the faults weren't **picked up** during the <u>field tests</u>.

這基本上是我們為了此車型所研發之新輕量化技術的一個面向。當然，這些瑕疵在實地測試時沒有被發現，我們感到很失望。

field test 指「實地測試、現場試驗」。

---

3. **structural** [ˈstrʌktʃərəl] *adj.* 結構的
The new CEO made several structural changes to the company.

字彙補給站

✽ **faulty** [ˈfɔlti] *adj.* 有缺陷的

✽ **derailleur** [dɪˈrelə] *n.* 變速器

✽ **rim** [rɪm] *n.* 輪圈

✽ **hub** [hʌb] *n.* 輪軸

 **Part C** 說明解決方案

 PLAY ALL ● TRACK 41

與會記者詢問自行車公司要如何解決相關問題。

R = Ralph   A = Alan   D = Dina   P = Patty

R: Can you give us any idea of what you're doing to **address**[1] the problems?

能否告訴我們，你們為解決問題所採取的措施？

A: Well, firstly, we have shipped all unsold bikes back to the warehouse, where the faults will be **corrected**.[2] We're confident we can **rectify**[3] the issue.

嗯，首先，我們已將所有未售出的自行車運回倉庫，那些瑕疵會就地進行修正。我們有信心能改正這次的問題。

> 指「想必、無疑地」，亦可用來表示驚訝，指「總不會……」。

D: <u>Surely</u> the **priority** is the consumers who have already purchased these bicycles?

想必首先要考慮的是已購買這些自行車的消費者吧？

Vocabulary

1. **address** [əˋdrɛs] *v.* 處理；應付
   To address the growing employee retention problem, the new CEO instituted an incentive program.

2. **correct** [kəˋrɛkt] *v.* 更正
   It is useless to point out a problem if you do not suggest a course of action to correct it.

P: Of course. We'll be offering all customers a refund of double what they paid to show how **seriously** we **take** this.

R: And if they like the bike and want to keep it?

於此指「強烈地；堅決地」。

A: We strongly **advise**[4] anyone who bought the Trekker 2000 to return the bike and receive the refund. We need the bikes back so we can make the necessary adjustments.

意思為「（尤指因為對購買的產品或服務不滿意而追回的）退款」。

adjustment 指「調整」，常搭配動詞 make，「微調」則可說 minor adjustment。

當然。我們將提供所有顧客其所付金額的兩倍退款，以展現我們非常認真看待這件事。

那如果他們喜歡這輛自行車而想留著呢？

我們強烈建議任何購買奇航者 2000 的人將車子送回並收取退款。我們需要回收這些自行車，才能做必要的調整。

---

3. **rectify** [ˈrɛktəˌfaɪ] v. 改正；矯正
At the press conference, the spokesman said they were taking the necessary steps to rectify the situation.

4. **advise** [ədˈvaɪz] v. 勸告；告知
The government advised consumers to be wary of products containing the dangerous ingredient.

Part D 說明因應措施

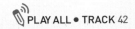 PLAY ALL • TRACK 42

自行車公司代表向記者們說明未來的因應措施。

 R = Ralph   A = Alan   D = Dina   P = Patty

avoid [əˋvɔɪd] 指「規避；逃避」。

R: It's all very well to throw money at the problem, but aren't you just <u>avoiding</u> the real issue — you sold bikes that, in some cases, **resulted in** <u>injuries</u>?

花錢解決事情是不錯，但你們是不是在規避真正的問題——你們賣的自行車在某些情況下導致受傷的情形？

injury [ˋɪndʒərɪ] 為名詞，指「傷害、損傷」，可搭配 receive、sustain 等動詞來表示「受傷」。

Vocabulary

1. **regret** [rɪˋgrɛt]
   v. 遺憾；為……感到抱歉
   Henry regretted that he wasn't living up to the potential that his mentor saw in him.

2. **attempt** [əˋtɛmpt] v. 嘗試；企圖（+ to）
   The company changed the tone of its advertising, attempting to lure a younger demographic.

A: Of course we sincerely **regret**[1] those, but we certainly aren't **attempting**[2] to **buy our way out of this.**

我們當然對那些狀況深表遺憾，但我們絕對沒有要花錢消災的意思。

> 讀做 [rɪˋkɝəns]，指「重演；復發」，
> 後面接介系詞 of 來帶出再次發生的事物。

D: How can you **guard against**[3] the recurrence of these types of PR disasters in the future?

你們未來要如何防範這類公關災難的重演？

> disaster [dɪˋzæstə] 指「災難、大禍」，常見搭配用法有：
> • be a disaster 非常失敗
> • spell disaster 意味著災難
> • recipe for disaster 災難的禍因

P: Disaster is a strong word. We've hired an independent QC agency, and all further QC and field tests will be recorded, with the video uploaded to our website.

用災難這個字眼太強烈了。我們已聘用獨立的品管機構，且日後所有的品管和實地測試都將錄影，影片則會上傳至我們的網站。

A: You can find the latest information there, too. Thank you again for coming.

你們也能在那裡看到最新資訊。再次感謝各位的蒞臨。

---

3. **guard against** [gɑrd] *v.* 防範；防止
New physical security measures were implemented to guard against intellectual property theft.

重點筆記

1. *make it* 到達

說明	make it 的常見意思有:

Ⓐ 到達、抵達（對話用法）
If we don't leave right now, we won't make it to the airport in time.
如果我們不立刻出發，我們就無法及時趕到機場。

Ⓑ 成功
When Cora was offered a job at the best university in the country, she knew she had made it.
當蔻拉在全國最好的大學覓得職位時，她就知道她成功了。

Ⓒ 存活、生存
The doctor wasn't sure if the man would make it after receiving so many injuries in a car accident.
醫生不確定這名在車禍中多處受傷的男子能否活下來。

2. *get down to business* 討論正題

說明	此慣用語形容「進入正題；開始辦正事」。business 在此指「所要討論的基本事項」，可用 brass tacks、the nitty-gritty、the nuts and bolts 等替換。

• Paul loathes the small talk in meetings and can't wait to get down to business.
保羅討厭開會時的閒聊，等不及要討論正題了。

3. *in a nutshell* 簡要地說

說明	此語以將許多複雜的東西濃縮在小核果（nutshell）裡來比喻「簡要、概括地說」。

• To put it in a nutshell, Brett realized he needed to start performing better at work.
簡單來説，布萊特意識到他得開始在工作上表現得更好。

4. *stem from* 源自；由⋯⋯造成

說明	stem [stɛm] 原本是植物的「莖；柄；梗」，當動詞時則指「起源於」，常與 from 連用，表示某事物的結果「源自」某原因。

- The delay in Harry's work stemmed from his poor time management.
  哈利工作延誤是他時間管理不善所造成。

5. *slip through the net* 漏掉

說明	此俚語以字面義「從網中滑出」引申指「漏網；被漏掉」。

- Once again the robbers have slipped through the police net.
  盜賊又一次逃離了警方所布下的天羅地網。

6. *pick up* 注意到；察覺

說明	pick up 的常見意思有：

Ⓐ 注意到；察覺（對話用法）

The crime scene investigator picked up on the strange blood splatter pattern.
該犯罪現場調查員注意到奇怪的飛濺血跡模式。

Ⓑ 改善；好轉

Credit demand in India is set to pick up in Q4, according to the government.
印度政府表示，其國內第四季的信貸需求將有所改善。

Ⓒ 習得；學會

The best way to pick up a language is to live in the country where people speak it.
學習語言最好的方式就是住在使用該語言的國家。

7. *priority* 優先考慮的事

| 說明 | priority [praɪˋɔrəti] 指「優先考慮的事」，常見的搭配用法有： |

Ⓐ **first/top priority** 首要考量
Since taking over as director of business development, Dan has made accountability his top priority.
自從接下事業發展部協理一職，丹就將責任視為首要之務。

Ⓑ **give priority to** 優先考慮
For upper-level staff openings, the company hires from within, giving priority to senior employees.
針對高階員工的職缺，該公司從內部徵聘，優先考慮資深員工。

Ⓒ **take priority over** 將……置於之前
Official business requirements obviously take priority over personal requests.
公務顯然要置於個人需求之前。

Ⓓ **get one's priorities straight** 優先處理最重要的事
Jenny really has to learn to get her priorities straight.
珍妮真的得學會優先處理最重要的事。

8. *take sb/sth seriously* 認真看待某人事物

| 說明 | 副詞 seriously 表示「認真地；嚴肅地」，take sb/sth seriously 即指「重視某人事物」，反義片語為 take sb/sth lightly「輕忽某人事物」。 |

- Gilbert doesn't take his job very seriously, so he will probably get fired.
吉伯特不太把他的工作當一回事，所以他可能會被開除。

- Although the sportswear brand was much more successful than its rivals, it didn't take them lightly.
儘管該運動服品牌比其競爭對手都來得成功，卻沒有因而輕忽對手。

9. *all very well* 還行、還不錯

說明	形容某事物在某些情況下還算可以，但不是都盡如人意，替換說法為 all well and good。

- Working hard is all very well, but occasional rest and relaxation keeps one healthy and happy.
  努力工作是沒錯，但是偶爾的休息和放鬆能保持健康愉快。

10. *throw money at* 花錢在……

說明	此片語的使用情境為某人相信只有錢才能解決問題。

- The CEO refused to solve the R & D problem just by throwing money at it.
  執行長拒絕只靠撒錢來解決這個研發的問題。

11. *result in* 導致；結果造成

說明	result 可當動詞，後接介系詞 in 來表示「造成……的結果」；若接 from 則指「起因於……；由……產生」。

- Hard work and a good attitude resulted in Janet getting a promotion.
  努力工作和好的態度讓珍妮特獲得升遷。

- Most car accidents result from people not paying attention to the road.
  多數的汽車事故起因於人們不注意路況。

12. *buy one's way out of sth* 花錢消災

說明	此俚語形容為了逃避或避免不愉快的事情而付錢，意近中文的「花錢消災」。

- By hiring the best legal counsel in the country, the mobster was able to buy his way out of prison.
  藉由聘請全國最棒的法律顧問，該匪徒得以免除牢獄之災。

5-2 Annual Plan Reports
年度企畫報告

年度企畫必備詞彙 & 實用句 PLAY ALL

 Fiscal Year 會計年度

actuals [ˈæktʃəwəlz]
實際營收

calculation [ˌkælkjəˈleʃən]
計算

projection [prəˈdʒɛkʃən]
預測

revenue forecast
[ˈrɛvəˌnju] [ˈfɔrˌkæst]
營收預測

- We're projecting that this year's revenue will increase by **10 percent** from 2019 actuals.
  我們預估今年的營收會比 2019 年的實際營收增加 10%。

- We'll be expected to bring in **US$5 million** in revenue this year.
  我們預期今年會帶來五百萬美元的營收。

Expansion Plans 拓展計畫

branch out [bræntʃ]
擴張

expand [ɪkˈspænd]
拓展

diversify [daɪˈvɜsəˌfaɪ]
多樣化經營

establish presence
建立能見度

- We're aiming to expand into **the southeast market**.
  我們計畫要拓展到東南區的市場。

- We're also considering opening up new offices in **North America**.
  我們也在考慮於北美設置新辦事處。

Ongoing Projects 進行中的企畫案

behind/on schedule
進度落後／如期

delay [dɪˋle]
延遲

underway [ˌʌndɚˋwe]
進行中的

- Not only is the work on the new project taking far longer than expected, it is coming in way over budget.

  新企畫案除了所花的時間遠超出預期，預算也嚴重超支。

- There have been a few cost overruns and delays on the Anderson Project.

  安德森企畫案一直有些經費超支和延誤的情形。

Budget 預算

cutback [ˋkʌtˌbæk]
節省開支

overrun [ˋovɚˌrʌn]
超支

- Spending is projected to increase 15 percent to US$30 million.

  花費預計增加 15% 至三千萬美元。

- The Canadian division is budgeted at US$20 million for the fiscal year.

  加拿大事業部在這個會計年度的預算為兩千萬美元。

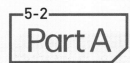

Part A 報告公司願景

美髮沙龍店的老闆蘇珊（Susan）
向合夥人菲力普（Phillip）和溫蒂
（Wendy）提出改變經營的方式以
增加客源……

S = Susan　　P = Phillip　　W = Wendy

S: Good morning. I've called you here today to talk about the future of this company. With our five-year anniversary* approaching, I think it'd be a good idea to **shake things up** a bit.

I've always wanted us to be the best in the biz, but we've never managed to beat out the other salons in the area. I'd like us to find a way to finally **come out on top**. We need to think about taking our salons in a different direction.

早安。我今天找你們來是要談談公司的未來。在我們五週年紀念來臨之際，我認為做些改變會是個好主意。

我一直都希望我們能成為業界的佼佼者，但我們從未成功擊敗過這個地區的其他美髮沙龍。我希望我們能找到方法來脫穎而出。我們得考慮將我們的沙龍店帶往不同的方向。

Vocabulary

1. **intrigue** [ɪnˈtrig]
   v. 激起……的好奇心或興趣
   The information in the article really intrigued Gary.

2. **integrate** [ˈɪntəˌgret] v. 整合；結合
   Carla tried to integrate more Asian elements in her clothing designs.

P: What do you mean?

S: Well, all of our competitors offer the same exact services, so what if we offered something they don't?

W: I'm **intrigued**.[1] Go on.

S: What if we **integrated**[2] some services that you would find in a traditional spa? Like massages and facials.*

P: But there are already several spas in town. How are we going to be able to compete with them?

S: The same way we'll **compete**[3] with salons. We'll be the only one-stop-shop* in town for all of one's beauty needs. I've done a lot of research on this, and I think it's the best way to ensure a successful future for us.

W: Well, I'm **sold**.

P: Sounds good.

S: Great. Now we'll **put** the plan **into action**!

你的意思是？

嗯，我們所有的競爭者都提供完全相同的服務，那麼如果我們提供一些他們沒有的東西呢？

你引起我的興趣了。請繼續說。

假使我們整合一些在傳統芳療找得到的服務呢？像是按摩和臉部保養。

但是城區已有幾間芳療館了。我們如何才能與他們競爭？

如同我們將跟其他沙龍競爭的方式。我們將成為此地區唯一一間能滿足所有美容需求的一站式店家。我在這方面已做了相當多的研究，我認為這是確保我們未來能成功的最好方法。

嗯，你說服我了。

聽起來不錯。

太好了。那我們就將計畫化為行動吧！

---

3. **compete** [kəm`pit] *v.* 與……競爭
   The tech company launched a new line of tablet computers to compete with the iPad.

字彙補給站

＊ **anniversary** [ˌænə`vɜsəri] *n.* 週年紀念

＊ **facial** [`feʃəl] *n.* 臉部美容

＊ **one-stop-shop** [`wʌn`stɑp`ʃɑp] *n.* 一站式消費商店

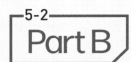

蘇珊與合夥人討論該如何落實美髮
沙龍店的新計畫……

P = Phillip　　S = Susan　　W = Wendy

P: Now that you've presented your idea, how do you propose we make it a reality?

S: I think the first logical step is to decide whether to make changes to our current locations or find new **properties**¹ to rent.

W: I think it would be a mistake to **relocate**² our shops. We could potentially <u>anger</u> lots of our long-term customers.

既然你已提出構想，你會怎麼建議我們付諸實踐？

我認為合理的第一步在於決定是否要改裝我們目前的店面，或另尋新的租賃物件。

我認為搬遷店面會是個錯誤。我們可能因此激怒許多長期顧客。

讀做 [ˈæŋɡɚ]，為動詞，指「激怒；使生氣」。

Vocabulary

1. **property** [ˈprɑpɚti]
   n. 房地產；所有物
   This small house is my only property.

2. **relocate** [riˈloˌket] *v.* 搬遷；遷移
   Some companies are thinking about relocating their factories to South America because of low labor costs there.

S: I agree with you **to a degree**, Wendy. While moving all of our locations wouldn't **make sense**, a good **course of action** would be to open one new place for our first salon/spa. That'll give us a chance to see which services are **hits**[3] and which are **duds**[4] before pouring a lot of money into the project.

P: Good idea.

W: OK. That sounds good. Now what about staff?

S: We should hire from within as much as possible. There may be employees at our salons now that have experience with certain types of spa treatments. Before looking for outside help, we should post job advertisements in our shops asking for people qualified to perform the services we want to provide.

P: That's an excellent idea.

W: We should also ask for suggestions from the staff, just in case we miss something.

S: Right. You know, I have a very good feeling about this!

溫蒂，我在一定程度上同意你的看法。儘管遷移我們所有的營業據點並不合理，但好的行動方針應該是找個新地點來開設我們的第一家沙龍芳療館。在投入大筆資金於這項企畫案以前，我們將有機會了解哪些服務是成功的，而哪些是沒有效益的。

好主意。

好的。聽起來很不錯。那員工的部分呢？

我們應該盡可能從內部做調動。目前我們的沙龍裡可能有員工具有某些類型的芳療療程經驗。在尋求外部幫助之前，我們應該在各分店張貼徵才廣告，找尋有資格的人選來執行我們想提供的服務。

那真是個很棒的主意。

我們應該也徵求員工們的建議，以防有什麼是我們遺漏掉的。

沒錯。你知道嗎，我對這項計畫很有信心！

---

3. **hit** [hɪt] *n.* 成功；風行一時的事物
Angelina's new movie is expected to be a big hit when it is released in Taiwan next month.

4. **dud** [dʌd] *n.* 無用、失敗之物
The meeting was a dud as far as new business was concerned.

重點筆記

1. *shake things up* 改變；更動現狀

說明	shake sth up 指「（通常為做出改進）對……進行大改組或大調整」，shake things up 即形容「改變；更動現狀」。

- **The Democrats are unlikely to shake things up hugely.**
  民主黨不太可能大幅改變現狀。

2. *come out on top* 脫穎而出；贏得勝利

說明	top 在此做「頂點；首位」解，come out on top 則形容打敗其他對手，從競爭中「脫穎而出；贏得勝利」。

- **If our new line is a hit, we'll come out on top in the industry.**
  如果我們的新系列產品很受歡迎，我們就能在業界拔得頭籌。

3. *I'm sold.* 你說服我了。

說明	sell 在口語中可表示「就事物的價值來說服別人、讓別人信服」。被動式的 I'm sold. 即指「我被說服了」。

- **This plan won't cost too much to implement, and the benefits to us could be massive. I'm sold.**
  這個計畫的執行成本不會太高，且帶給我們的效益可能很大。我被你說服了。

4. *put into action* 採取實際行動

說明	action 是「行動；行為」的意思，put into action 即表示「將……付諸實行」。

- **The rescuers put their plan into action.**
  救援人員將他們的計畫付諸實行。

5. *to a degree* 在某種程度上

說明	此片語的 **degree** 之前可加上 great、large、small 等形容詞，表示程度的高低。

- This project has been successful to a degree that none of us thought possible.
  這個專案的成功程度是我們始料未及的。

- How much money a person earns depends, to a great degree, on his or her level of education.
  一個人的收入多寡，在很大程度上，取決於他的教育程度。

6. *make sense* 合理；有道理

說明	**make sense** 在此指「有道理；合乎情理」，也可指某事物有明確的意義。相關用法 **make sense of sth** 則指「理解、懂得某事」。

- It makes sense to check your car's oil before a long road trip.
  長途旅行之前先檢查車子用油是很合理的。

- Can you make sense of these strange characters carved in the stone?
  你看得懂刻在石頭上的這些奇怪文字嗎？

7. *course of action* 行動方針；因應之道

說明	本片語形容為因應某特殊情況而做的處理。

- The company president must decide on a course of action to take during slow economic times.
  該公司總裁必須決定經濟成長緩慢時期所須採行的對策。

5-3 A Guiding Vision
發展策略報告

制定策略實用方法 & 應用句 🔊 PLAY ALL

Identifying a company's SWOT traits
辨識公司的 SWOT 特質

What strengths do we have?
我們有什麼優勢？

· We have a reputable market presence, stores in prime locations, and two successful online sales platforms.

我們有信譽良好的市場地位、位於黃金地點的店面以及兩個成功的網路銷售平台。

What weaknesses do we have?
我們有什麼劣勢？

· We have a weak relationship with younger consumers and our workforce is much too unstable, both due to an outdated business objective.

我們和年輕消費者的關係薄弱，且我們的員工組成太不穩定了，兩者都是過時的經營目標所致。

What opportunities do we have?
我們有什麼機會？

· Our analytical marketing team has identified underexploited market trends, as well as possibilities for mergers and strategic alliances.

我們的分析行銷團隊已找出開發不足的市場趨勢，以及合併與策略聯盟的可能性。

What kind of threats might we encounter?
我們可能遇到什麼樣的威脅？

· It's a race to stay ahead of several strong competitors; meanwhile, our stakeholders are wary of changing tack.

保持領先強勁的對手是場硬仗，同時，我們的股東對變更的行動方針格外小心。

Applying the USED skills to formulate strategies
運用 USED 技巧制定策略

How can we use each strength?
我們能如何善用每個優勢？

· In addition to updating the brand image, we will also continue to strengthen customer traffic across all platforms.

除了更新品牌形象，我們也將繼續鞏固所有平台的顧客流量。

How can we stop each weakness?
我們能如何終止每個劣勢？

· As well as looking at future demands, we also have projects underway to help facilitate employee retention.

除了著眼未來需求，我們也在進行能促進員工留任的計畫。

How can we exploit each opportunity?
我們能如何開發每個機會？

· Joint ventures have proven to be effective, as they correctly align with our mission goals of enlarging our profit margins.

合資已證明是有效的，因為這樣做與我們擴大利潤的任務目標一致。

How can we defend against each threat?
我們能如何防禦每個威脅？

· We will continue to focus our efforts on claiming a leadership position in the industry, instilling confidence in our investors.

我們將繼續專注於爭取業界的領先地位，將信心灌輸於我們的投資人。

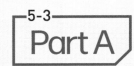

討論銷售業績

服裝品牌 Biz Chic 的執行長賽克瑞（Zachary）、總經理凱莉（Carrie）和行銷總監寇克（Kirk）開會討論公司的首季業績表現。

Z = Zachary　　C = Carrie　　K = Kirk

Z: All right, let's get down to business. What are the numbers for the first quarter?

好，我們進入正題吧。第一季的數據如何？

C: The good news is, we met the overall sales goal of 150 million NT.

好消息是，我們達到新台幣 1.5 億元的整體銷售目標。

Z: And the bad news?

那壞消息是？

C: The revenue stream is continuously <u>uneven</u> in <u>distribution</u>. Several clothing lines are just not **budging**[1] from the shelves.

銷售部分的營收來源一直都不平均。幾個服裝系列就是無法從架上賣出去。

讀做 [ˌdɪstrəˈbjuʃən]，指「銷售（量）」。

讀做 [ʌnˈivən]，指「不平均的」。

Vocabulary

1. **budge** [bʌdʒ] *v.* 移動
   Despite urging the horse onward repeatedly, Elsie found that her mount refused to budge.

2. **worrisome** [ˈwɝisəm] *adj.* 令人擔憂的
   It's a worrisome state of affairs in that boardroom: three alliances have formed, and no one is willing to compromise.

K: Sales pick up after a marketing **push** but soon **lose** their **momentum**. This is especially obvious in <u>brick-and-mortar</u> stores.

> 讀做 [͵brɪkən`mɔrtə]，指「實體的」，意義相對的為 vital「虛擬的」。

行銷推廣活動後，銷售曾有起色，但很快又失去成長動力。這在實體店面尤其明顯。

Z: Hmm. You also mentioned there is a <u>staffing</u> issue.

> 指「與員工有關的」，如 staffing level「人員編制」、staffing shortage「人員短缺」。

嗯，你還提到人員編制的問題。

K: There is a **worrisome**[2] **turnover**[3] in sales clerks and customer service agents. I think a <u>rebranding</u> would **address**[4] both problems.

> 指「給（品牌、公司、產品等）重塑形象」。

店員和客服專員的流動率令人擔憂。我想重塑品牌形象應該能解決這些問題。

---

3. **turnover** [`tɜn͵ovə] *n.* 流動率
We have a very high turnover of food at our café, so freshness is always guaranteed.

4. **address** [ə`drɛs] *v.* 處理；應對
The management needs to seriously address the issue of sexual harassment in our company before we lose more employees.

Part B 討論促銷構想

三人接著討論如何刺激系列服飾的
銷量。

Z = Zachary　　C = Carrie　　K = Kirk

Z: Carrie, I want you to identify where we can **cut our losses** by pulling clothing lines that are <u>flat-out</u> duds.

> 讀做 [`flæt͵aʊt`]，
> 指「完全的」，
> 用於強調的情境。

> nix [nɪks] 指「停止；
> 拒絕」。

凱莉，我要你抽掉完全沒銷量的系列，確認我們可減少哪些損失。

C: Sure. **In addition to** <u>nixing</u> merchandise, I'll **cull**[1] market research for what we can **salvage**[2] by adjusting the designs.

好的。除了停止商品販售，我還將收集市調結果，看看我們可用調整設計來挽救什麼。

Vocabulary

1. **cull** [kʌl] *v.* 收集；揀選
NBA scouts often cull new players by attending college basketball tournaments, which often adds extra tension to the games.

2. **salvge** [`sælvɪdʒ`] *v.* 挽救
Before anyone could stop her, Shirley darted into the burning house, determined to salvage the Monet painting.

K: I'd like to **spearhead**[3] **revamping**[4] the brand's look and feel to <u>unify</u> our stores, websites, and packaging.

> 口語用法,指「極佳的,非常好的」。

> 讀做 [ˈjunəˌfaɪ],指「統一;整合」。

Z: <u>Splendid</u>. I'll expect <u>case studies</u> of trending styles and labels, plus anticipating future demand.

> case study 指「(為說明一般原則而做的)個案研究」。

K: Do we want to copy what's hot at the moment?

C: I say copy what's becoming hot, so we're a step ahead. That'll draw sales from current and new customers.

我想負責改造品牌的樣貌與氛圍,藉此統一店面、網站以及包裝。

太好了。我期待看到的個案研究是能走在潮流上的風格與品牌,而且可預測未來的需求。

我們要仿效目前最熱門的設計嗎?

我會說是仿效即將變熱門的設計,我們才得以領先一步。那將能從現有和新的顧客那裡帶來銷量。

---

3. **spearhead** [ˈspɪrˌhɛd]
   v. 領導(行動);帶頭做

   Today, I'd like to assign individuals to spearhead each effort and report back on their progress in a week.

4. **revamp** [riˈvæmp] *v.* 改造

   The new president of the college has put a lot of effort into revamping the school's international image.

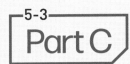 **Part C** 討論人事問題

三人討論減少公司員工流失率的可行方法。

K = Kirk   Z = Zachary   C = Carrie

K： We must decrease our staff turnover rate to below 20 percent for anyone at or above assistant manager level.

我們必須將任何協理級或以上職等的員工流失率降至兩成以下。

Z： No higher than 20 percent **across the board**. Why are we losing so many people?

所有職等的員工都不能超過兩成。為什麼我們流失這麼多人？

K： Again, it's the lack of a strong brand identity that people would feel loyalty toward. And financial <u>incentives</u> wouldn't hurt.

還是那句老話，就是缺少讓人有向心力的強烈品牌認同。可試試看財務方面的鼓勵。

incentive [ɪnˋsɛntɪv] 指「鼓勵；激勵」。

Vocabulary

1. **arm** [ɑrm] *v.* 提供；準備
   After a few coaching sessions with his lawyer, Gordon walked into the meeting armed with a clear objective.

2. **retain** [rɪˋten] *v.* 留住；保留
   If you really want to retain any of this information in the future, cramming it in one go won't work.

C: I **vote for** a training program to **arm**[1] employees with better <u>appreciation</u> of our products.

我贊成能讓員工更了解公司產品的培訓計畫。

> 讀做 [əˌpriʃìˋeʃən]，
> 指「理解；欣賞」。

Z: OK, but to really **retain**[2] people, it's time we expanded the <u>stock ownership program</u> to anyone who's been with us for two years.

好，但真要留住人，是擴大持股計畫的時候了，讓任職達兩年的任何員工都能加入。

> stock ownership program「持股計畫」的正式名稱為 employee stock ownership plans (ESOP)，指企業為留任或激勵員工，而讓他們持有股票，使其獲得利益並參與相關經營決策。

C: Is it **viable**[3] to also **reinstate**[4] the sales bonus incentive?

恢復銷售獎金也是可行的吧？

---

3. **viable** [ˋvaɪəbəl] *adj.* 可實行的
The VP liked your idea of contacting firms in Vietnam, so it looks like a viable option in the near future.

4. **reinstate** [ˌriənˋstet] *v.* 恢復；使復職
The mayor's office formally apologized to the former treasurer, but there is no word on whether he'll be reinstated.

三人最後商討公司接下來的發展策略。

C = Carrie　　K = Kirk　　Z = Zachary

C: We still need to address our overall operating strategies for the rest of 2016. Is the <u>differentiation approach</u> working?

我們仍需要處理這一年接下來的整體營運策略。差異化手法有效嗎？

指「差異化手法」，形容利用公司的自身優勢與消費者的偏好，做出自家產品與其他類似商品的市場區隔，使自家商品變得更有吸引力。

Vocabulary

1. **justify** [ˈdʒʌstəˌfaɪ]
   v. 證明……是合理的
   It's hard to say if we'll cut the number of stores this year, but the question justifies consideration.

2. **narrowly** [ˈnɛroli] adv. 嚴密地；狹義地
   I am speaking about the affected population narrowly, as in, only those people who directly suffered from the typhoon.

K: Quality is our major **bargaining chip**, so it **justifies**[1] a cost that falls in the market's higher <u>bracket</u>.

> 讀做 [ˋbrækət]，指「階層；等級」。

品質是我們的主要籌碼，所以價格落在市場的較高層級是合理的。

C: But **with the exception of** wealthy customers, that justification **falls on deaf ears**. We need to shift to <u>focus strategies</u>.

> focus strategy「重點戰略」指企業擬定策略以迎合特定消費族群的需要，或集中某一個區域市場，從而取得優勢和競爭地位。

但除了富裕的顧客，那樣的理由是不會被理睬的。我們得轉移到重點戰略。

Z: Yes, promote high-end goods **narrowly**.[2] However, I'm also after <u>batch</u> sales this year — say, **lucrative**[3] contracts for designer uniforms.

> 讀做 [bætʃ]，指「一批」。

是的，要嚴密推銷高檔商品。不過我也贊成今年做大批銷售，像是能帶來豐厚利潤的設計款制服合約。

K: I have a **pertinent**[4] contact at city hall. Should I set up a meeting for next week?

我在市政府有認識的人。下星期我該安排會議嗎？

---

3. **lucrative** [ˋlukrətɪv] *adj.* 有利可圖的
   Michael couldn't refuse the lucrative job offer in Luxembourg, but it was hard to leave his aging parents behind.

4. **pertinent** [ˋpɝtənənt] *adj.* 有關的
   The police set up a hotline, welcoming anyone with pertinent information regarding the case to phone it in.

重點筆記

1. *push* 推銷；宣傳

說明	push 當名詞除了指「推擠」，也有其他以下的意思：

Ⓐ 推銷；宣傳（對話用法）

- The movie is unlikely to attract large audiences unless it is given a big push in the media.
  除非在媒體中大肆宣傳，否則這部電影不大可能吸引大批觀眾。

Ⓑ（生意上為贏得優勢而進行的）努力

- The hostel is making a major push to attract customers.
  這家民宿正在大搞活動以吸引顧客。

Ⓒ 鼓勵

- My father had always wanted to learn how to play the guitar; he just needed a push.
  我父親一直想學彈吉他，他只是需要有人鼓勵他一下。

2. *lose momentum* 失去動力

說明	momentum [moˋmɛntəm] 指「動力」，常搭配 lose「失去」或 gain「獲得」等動詞使用，相關片語 ride the momentum 則指「趁著氣勢」。

- I'm not sure why the company lost momentum halfway through last year.
  我不確定為什麼該公司去年中途就失去了成長動力。

- The director hopes the trilogy's final installment will ride the momentum of the first two films' box office success.
  導演希望此三部曲的最後一集能搭上前兩集票房成功的氣勢。

3. *cut one's losses* 減少損失

說明	cut loss 是投資領域的專有名詞，即所謂的「停損」，形容投資失利時，要及時認賠出場，才不會虧損地更嚴重。cut one's losses 即指「減少損失」。相關用法還有 suffer losses「蒙受損失」和 at a loss「虧本地；賠本地」。

- You should try to cut your losses when the situation doesn't look promising.
  情況看來不妙的時候，你就應該設法減少自己的損失。

- Many businesses suffered huge losses as a result of the typhoon.
  許多公司行號因颱風而蒙受鉅額損失。

- We are selling last year's models at a loss.
  我們賠錢出售去年的款式。

4. *in addition to* 除了……之外

說明	in addition to 為介系詞片語，後面接名詞或 V-ing。意思和用法相同的介系詞還有 besides、apart from、aside from 等。

- In addition to computers, this company also makes cell phones.
  除了電腦之外，該公司也製造手機。

- Besides winning a trophy, Ken ended up with a large amount of prize money.
  除了贏得獎盃，肯恩最後還獲得一大筆獎金。

- Apart from his success as a businessman, Warren Buffett is also well known for his charity work.
  除了是個成功的企業家，華倫‧巴菲特也因他的慈善工作而廣為人知。

5. *across the board* 全面地

board 的單字解釋為「硬質板；公告板」，來看看與 board 連用的片語：

Ⓐ across the board 全面地

- With a change of leadership, the corporation's fortunes improved across the board.
  隨著領導階層的更替，這家企業的際遇獲得全面的改善。

Ⓑ get sb on board 使某人接受（建議、想法等）

- The president must get congress on board if he wants to pass his budget proposal.
  總統若想通過其預算提案，他就得說服國會。

Ⓒ go by the board （計畫、安排等）落空

- Plans for a new park went by the board when the city ran out of money.
  新公園的計畫在市政府用完經費後落空了。

6. *vote for sth* 對某事物投贊成票

vote 指「投票；進行表決」，常見的用法整理如下：

Ⓐ vote for / in favor of 投票支持……（對話用法）

- Mike voted in favor of the new company policy because it would help make his job easier.
  麥克投票支持新的公司政策，因為那會讓他的工作更輕鬆。

Ⓑ vote against 投票反對……

- Patty voted against this politician in the last election.
  派蒂在上次的選舉中對這名政治人物投下了反對票。

Ⓒ vote on sth 對某事物進行表決

- Let's vote on whether to have a dress code in the office or not.
  我們來投票表決辦公室是否要訂定服裝規定。

7. *bargaining chip* 談判籌碼

說明	bargaining [ˋbɑrgənɪŋ] 指「交涉；講價」，chip 則指「（玩撲克牌時用的）籌碼」，bargaining chip 即形容談判時做為退讓條件或威脅的事物。

- Access to natural resources often becomes a bargaining chip between countries engaged in conflict.
  自然資源的取得常成為衝突國家之間的談判籌碼。

8. *with the exception of* 除了……之外

說明	名詞 exception [ɪkˋsɛpʃən] 指「例外；例外的人事物」，with the exception of 即表示「除了……之外」。與 exception 連用的片語還有 be no exception「……也不例外」和 make an exception「破例」。

- Teddy likes all kinds of movies with the exception of comedies.
  除了喜劇片之外，各種電影泰迪都喜歡。

- Some people find it difficult to understand complex math problems, and I am no exception.
  有些人覺得複雜的數學問題難以理解，而我也不例外。

- I don't really drink alcohol, but I make an exception on special occasions.
  我不太喝酒，但在特別場合我會破例。

9. *fall on deaf ears* 未被理睬

說明	deaf [dɛf] 指「耳聾的」。此片語以事物為主詞，引申形容某建議或意見「不受注意；被忽視」。類似含意的片語為 turn a deaf ear「充耳不聞；不理會」。

- I tried to tell Jeff how to improve his paper, but my advice fell on deaf ears.
  我試著告訴傑夫要怎麼改進他的論文，但是我的意見不被理睬。

- People are always asking Gavin for help, and sometimes he has to turn a deaf ear.
  大家總是找蓋文幫忙，有時候他得充耳不聞。

5-4 Presenting Company Outlook

年度展望報告

說明圖表好用句 🖑 PLAY ALL

Line Graph 折線圖

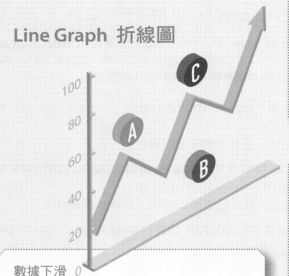

數據上揚

If Q1 trend of steadily climbing sales repeats, our initial outlook is pretty bright.

如果第一季銷量穩定爬升的趨勢能重現,我們的初步展望相當看好。

數據下滑

However, we need to avoid repeating last year's plummet in sales during Q2.

然而,我們得避免重演去年第二季業績驟降的情況。

數據持平

As Q3 is our slower season, we need to ensure that our numbers remain at an acceptable plateau.

由於第三季是我們的淡季,我們得確保業績數字維持在可接受的持平水準。

數據波動

We have to take precautions to prevent the frenetic fluctuations in sales which occurred during last year's Q4.

我們必須採取預防措施,避免去年第四季業績劇烈波動的情形。

Bar Graph 長條圖

數據攀升

Compared to 2018, our international sales in 2019 have progressively shown marked improvement with each quarter.

與 2018 年相比，我們 2019 年的外銷，每季都有顯著的成長。

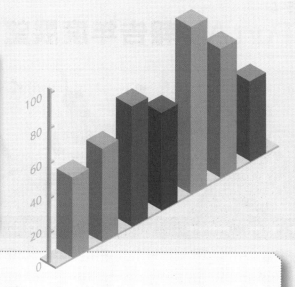

數據走跌

However, 2019 saw a drastic drop in domestic sales, with numbers consistently lower than 2018 across all four quarters.

然而，2019 年的內銷卻大幅下滑，四個季度的銷售數字一致比 2018 年的都低。

Pie Chart 圓餅圖

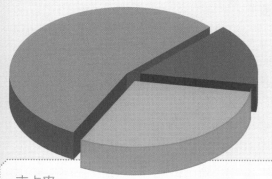

整體表現

This pie chart depicts the domestic market shares of our company in comparison with our competitors.

這張圓餅圖說明我們公司與競爭對手相較的國內市占率。

市占率

Our company holds a current market share of 38 percent, which is the second largest percentage.

我們公司目前擁有 **38%** 的市占率，占比為第二大。

報告年度展望

某電源供應器製造商的業務經理英格（Inga）向營運長古斯塔夫（Gustav）、研發經理布雷克（Blake）以及人資經理潘妮洛普（Penelope）報告公司的年度展望。

I = Inga G = Gustav P = Penelope B = Blake

I: Last year, we put up great domestic numbers, **commanding**[1] 56 percent of the market. However, our market shares in <u>population dense</u> **emerging**[2] nations, like Brazil and India, are <u>fairly</u> anemic:* only 12 percent.

讀做 [ˌpɑpjəˈlɛʃən] [dɛns]，指「人口密集的」。

讀做 [ˈfɛrli]，指「相當地；一定程度地」。

去年，我們大幅提高了國內的銷售數字，拿下 56% 的市場。然而，我們的市占率在巴西和印度等人口密集的新興國家相當低，只有 12%。

Vocabulary

1. **command** [kəˈmænd] *v.* 掌握；統率
   Our company commands a team of skilled tech experts.

2. **emerging** [ɪˈmɜdʒɪŋ] *adj.* 新興的
   Many emerging countries possess large income disparities.

G: Can we send some people out there to **get our foot in the door** and <u>schmooze</u>?

我們可以派人到那裡，踏出第一步並展開商談嗎？

UNIT
5
公司運作 ● 年度展望報告

讀做 [ʃmuz]，指「攀談；閒聊」。

P: We've got a few sales <u>veterans</u> who'd be perfect.

我們有幾個資深業務，應該會是完美人選。

veteran [ˋvɛtərən] 於此指「老手、經驗豐富的人」，另有「老兵；退伍軍人」的意思。

I: On a positive note, sales have gone up across the board since the launch of our newest generation of adapters.*

往好的一面看，自我們最新一代的轉接器上市後，業績就全面攀升了。

B: Glad to **be of service**.

很高興幫得上忙。

I: <u>Furthermore</u>, our growth outlook **predicts**[3] improvement of 30 percent over the next quarter.

此外，我們的成長前景預測下一季的增幅將達 30%。

讀做 [ˋfɝðə͵mɔr]，為副詞，指「此外、而且」。

---

3. **predict** [prɪˋdɪkt] *v.* 預測
Our analyst predicts that sales will double over Q4.

字彙補給站

* **anemic** [əˋnimɪk] *adj.* 沒有活力的
* **adapter** [əˋdæptə] *n.* 轉接器

Part B 討論新產品開發

古斯塔夫、布雷克以及英格接著討論公司新產品的研發。

G = Gustav　　B = Blake　　I = Inga

G: So what's the next product coming **down the line**?

那下一個要推出的產品是什麼？

B: We've been studying the competition so we can **one-up**[1] them. This bar graph shows a 12 percent increase in our largest competitor's market shares since last year.

我們一直在研究競爭對手，這樣才能贏過他們。這張長條圖顯示我們最大競爭者的市占率自去年增加了 12%。

G: They've <u>gone up</u>. Why so?

他們的市占數據成長了。為何會這樣？

go up 的常見意思有：
❶ 上升；增長（對話用法）
❷ 被建造起來
❸ 突然爆炸

Vocabulary

1. one-up [ˌwʌnˋʌp] *v.* 贏過；取得優勢
My competitive colleague always tries to one-up every idea I propose.

2. forefront [ˋforˌfrʌnt] *n.* 最重要的地位
Our team is at the forefront of technological advancement in the industry.

I: Because they **went green**, right? Consumer surveys show that <u>eco-friendliness</u> is at the **forefront**[2] of customer | **consciousness**.[3]

因為他們採取綠化政策，對吧？消費者調查顯示，環保是顧客意識中最被看重的一環。

> 字首 eco- 指「與環境有關的；生態的」，eco-friendliness 遂為「環保」的意思。

B: Precisely. We've **taken the bull by the horns** and **put our blood, sweat, and tears into** developing the most energy efficient adapter ever produced.

沒錯。我們不畏艱難，投注血汗和淚水，開發出有史以來最節能的轉接器。

G: When can we <u>expect</u> to enter production?

我們預計何時進入生產階段？

> 讀做 [ɪkˋspɛkt]，指「預計；預料」，常用句構為 expect + to V. 或 expect that + 子句。

B: I'm confident we can have it ready in two months.

我有信心我們能在兩個月內準備好。

---

3. **consciousness** [ˋkɑnʃəsnəs] *n.* 意識
Civic responsibility and social justice are usually big issues in the public consciousness.

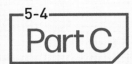
Part C 檢討人力問題

人資經理潘妮洛普向營運長古斯塔夫和業務經理英格報告公司的人力問題。

P = Penelope   I = Inga   G = Gustav

P: These figures show a 10 percent increase in our employee turnover last year. I suggest we re-examine our employee welfare* policies.

I: Skilled labor is **retained**[1] labor. Why not offer advanced training seminars?*

G: <u>That's doable.</u>

> 常用於口語中，替換説法為 That's feasible. 或 That's workable.。

這些數字顯示，去年我們的員工流動率增加了 10%。我建議我們重新檢視公司的員工福利政策。

有技能的勞工是得留住的勞動力。何不提供進階的培訓研討會？

那可行。

Vocabulary

1. retain [rɪˋten] v. 保留；保持
Good rest and frequent exercise can help you retain your focus for longer.

2. gauge [gedʒ] v. 判斷
I'm having trouble gauging whether the committee liked my proposal or not.

讀做 [kənˋdʌkt]，指「進行；實施」。

P: HR could <u>conduct</u> surveys to **gauge**² where employees require additional training.

人資可進行調查，判斷員工在哪些方面需要額外的培訓。

讀做 [gæp] 指「缺口」。
常見應用如下：
• labor gap　勞力缺口
• bridge the gap　彌合差距
• gap in the market　市場空白

G: Excellent. But how will we fill our labor <u>gap</u>?

太棒了。但我們要如何填補勞力缺口？

對話中的 bonus 指 employee referral
bonus「員工介紹獎金」。

P: We can offer <u>bonuses</u> to employees who **enlist**³ friends and family to work for us. This will **cut down on** recruitment* costs.

我們可提供介紹獎金給招攬朋友或家人來公司工作的員工。這會減少招募成本。

G: It'll grow our **sense of community**, too. I approve.

也將增進群體認同感。我贊成。

---

3. **enlist** [ɪnˋlɪst] v. 招攬
   We need to enlist more professionals with mathematical backgrounds to help design our new app.

字彙補給站

＊ **welfare** [ˋwɛl⸴fɛr] n. 福利

＊ **seminar** [ˋsɛmə⸴nɑr] n. 研討會

＊ **recruitment** [rɪˋkrutmənt] n. 招募

展望未來與總結

會議最後為公司的新年展望。

G = Gustav   I = Inga   B = Blake   P = Penelope

讀做 [ˈtɑpəvðəˈlaɪn]，指「（產品）頂級的、
最昂貴的」，意同 top-of-the-range。

G: We've got plans to expand our market, a
top-of-the-line product **in the works**, and
some <u>means</u> to keep employee **morale**[1]
high.

複數形的 means 指「方法、手段」，
「透過……的方法」可用 by means of 表示。

我們已有拓展市場的計畫，在
進行中的頂尖產品，以及一些
維持員工士氣高漲的方法。

Vocabulary

1. **morale** [məˈræl] *n.* 士氣
   Frequent breaks help to keep
   our employees' morale up.

2. **considerably** [kənˈsɪdərəbli] *adv.* 顯著地
   Productivity improved considerably after we
   purchased updated equipment.

I: We shouldn't **get too big for our britches**, though. The domestic market has slowed down **considerably**.[2]

但我們不該太過自信。國內市場已明顯趨緩了。

B: In an uncertain market, we can **hedge our bets** on **breaking new ground** in R & D.

在不確定的市場裡，我們可開創研發的新領域以分散風險。

G: Exactly! By launching our green adapter, we should gain an estimated 60 percent market share in the <u>aforementioned</u> developing markets.

沒錯！藉由推出綠能轉接器，我們應該能在前述的開發中市場取得 60% 的預估市占率。

> 讀做 [ˈæfɔrˈmɛnʃənd]，指「前面提到的；上述的」。

I: This'll **offset**[3] any projected losses.

這將會彌補任何預期的損失。

P: Additionally, a more skilled workforce will <u>soften</u> any domestic sales **blows**.[4]

此外，技能較完備的勞動力將緩和任何國內銷量的衝擊。

> 讀做 [ˈsɔfən]，為動詞，指「緩和；軟化」。

G: **From where I'm sitting**, 2017 looks like a big year for us.

就我看來，這一年會是我們大豐收的一年。

---

3. **offset** [ˈɔfˌsɛt] *v.* 彌補；抵銷
Working overtime will offset the time we lost due to the typhoon.

4. **blow** [blo] *n.* 衝擊
We received a serious blow to our reputation after the product recall.

重點筆記

1. *get one's foot in the door* 踏出第一步

說明	以下整理和 foot 連用的俚語：

Ⓐ get one's foot in the door　踏出第一步
- We got our foot in the door of the successful start-up before our competitors.
  我們搶在競爭對手前踏出成功創業的第一步。

Ⓑ put one's foot down　堅決阻止；堅持立場
- Theresa wants to buy a new car, but I'm putting my foot down and saying no.
  泰瑞莎想買新車，但是我要堅決阻止並說不行。

2. *on a positive note* 往好的一面看

說明	note 在此指「形式」；on a positive note 的替換說法有 on the bright side 和 in better news。

- The manager tries to conclude the discussion on a positive note.
  經理試著朝好的一面來總結這次的討論。

3. *be of service* 幫上忙

說明	service 指「服務；接待」，be of service 即形容「幫上忙」，類似說法為 do sb a service。

- These groceries look heavy. Perhaps I can be of service and carry them.
  這些雜貨看起來很重。或許我能幫忙搬。
- You've done me a great service on this proposal.
  你在這個提案上幫了我一個大忙。

4. *down the line* 未來；往後

說明	以字面義「沿著線下去」比喻「未來；一段時間後」，line 可用 road、track 等字替換。

- The company is planning on making some big changes down the line.
  該公司正計畫未來進行一些大幅度的改變。

5. *go green* 採取綠化政策

說明	此片語以環保的代表色「綠色」來形容「奉行環保原則」。

- I've decided to go green. From now on, I am going to walk to work.
  我決定要奉行環保原則。從現在起，我會走路去上班。

6. *take the bull by the horns* 不畏艱難

說明	字面意思是「抓住牛角」，而要正面抓住牛角是需要極大的勇氣和信心的，因此這個說法用來比喻「勇敢面對困難」或「當機立斷處理問題」。

- Rather than procrastinate, let's take the bull by the horns and finish the campaign now.
  與其拖延，我們別害怕艱難，現在就來完成這個活動吧。

7. *put sb's blood, sweat, and tears into* 付出諸多心力

說明	此俚語以字面義「投注血、汗及淚水」比喻「盡最大的努力」，put 可用 pour 替換。

- Bruce has poured his blood, sweat, and tears into this project.
  布魯斯為了這個專案付出諸多心力。

8. *cut down on* 減少

說明	cut down 指「消減；刪減」，後面接介系詞 on 來帶出欲減少的事物。替換說法有 scale down、trim down 等。

- Peter wants to cut down on the amount of coffee he drinks each day.
  彼得想要減少他每天喝的咖啡量。

9. *sense of community* 群體認同感

說明	要表達「……的感覺」，常用 a sense of + N. 的結構，對話中的 sense of community 即指「群體認同感」。其他常見的例子還有 sense of achievement「成就感」、sense of direction「方向感」、sense of humor「幽默感」等。

- Ryan felt a great sense of achievement when he finished building his boat.
  萊恩將船建造完成後很有成就感。

- I wish I had a better sense of direction. I'm always getting lost!
  但願我有更好的方向感。我老是迷路！

- Nick has a great sense of humor, so he's always fun to talk to.
  尼克有絕佳的幽默感，所以跟他說話總是很開心。

10. *in the works* 在進行中

說明	work 指「工作；勞動；作業」，in the works 即形容事情「在進行中；在準備中」。

- The country's plans to switch from 4G to 5G cellular technology are in the works.
  該國從 4G 轉換成 5G 手機技術的計畫正在進行中。

11. *get too big for one's britches* 過度自信

說明	britches [ˈbrɪtʃəz] 指「馬褲」，此俚語的字面義為「某人的馬褲尺寸過大」，後引申形容某人「過度自信」。

- Simon has been getting too big for his britches since he got that promotion.
  賽門自獲得升遷後就自大無比。

12. *hedge one's bets* （避免損失）分散風險

說明	hedge [hɛdʒ] 本身即指「兩面下注以避免（賭博等的）損失」，bet 則為「賭注」的意思，hedge one's bets 遂形容「為避免損失而兩邊都押寶」。

- Let's hedge our bets and invest our assets evenly among numerous lucrative prospects.
  讓我們分散風險，將資產平均投資在多項能獲利的標的裡。

13. *break new ground* 開創新局

說明	break ground 原指「（工程、工地）破土」，引申指「創辦；開始執行；著手」。break new ground 即表示「突破舊制、開創新局」。

- Tech companies need to continue to break new ground in order to stay ahead of the market.
  科技公司得持續開創新局才能走在市場前端。

14. *from where one's sitting* 就某人看來

說明	以字面義「從某人所坐的位置」來比喻「其個人的看法」，類似說法有 in one's opinion、as far as one is concerned。

- Our hiring options look pretty good from where I'm sitting.
  就我看來，我們能聘雇的人選都相當不錯。

UNIT
6

Company
Performances
營運表現

預算報告必備字彙 & 應用句 PLAY ALL

projected budget
[prə`dʒɛktəd] [`bʌdʒət]
預算

A projected budget is used to request next year's department funds.
一筆預算用來申請下一年度的部門經費。

budget allowance
[ə`lauəns]
預算津貼

We have no budget allowance for company outings this year.
我們今年沒有員工旅遊的預算津貼。

modified budget
[`madə͵faɪd]
變更預算

The unexpected departmental expense requires a modified budget.
這筆預料之外的部門支出需要變更預算。

allotment
[əˋlɑtmənt]
配額

We have used up this year's allotment of funds.
我們已用完今年的資金配額。

allocation
[ˌæləˋkeʃən]
配置

The budget allocation for our department is 30 percent higher this year.
我們部門的預算配置今年增加了三成。

cash flow
[kæʃ] [flo]
現金流；資金流轉

We are expecting improved cash flow for Q3.
我們預計第三季度的現金流將有所改善。

expenditure
[ɪkˋspɛndɪtʃə]
支出（額）

Please explain each expenditure on your financial report.
請說明財務報告裡的各項支出。

balance
[ˋbæləns]
結餘款項

The balance on the bill is still outstanding and needs to be paid.
帳單上的餘額仍未償還，得結清才行。

6-1
Part A 營收報告

🔖 PLAY ALL ● TRACK 53

簡報者首先分析公司的主要營收來源與消長情形……

S = Speaker

S: Good afternoon. Now that everyone is here, I will go ahead and begin my presentation for our annual budget.

午安。既然所有人都到齊了，我就直接開始簡報公司的年度預算了。

> 讀做 [ˋstægnənt]，指「停滯的」。

As you can see, our budget remained constant while our growth was <u>stagnant</u>. However, it has been increased slightly over the past few quarters in large part due to our recent push for expansion through the Midwest region.

如你們所見，我們的預算維持不變，而我們的成長停滯。然而，前幾季出現小幅度的成長，絕大部分是由於我們近來積極拓展中西部的業務。

Our projected budget for next year is expected to increase by a similar percentage as last year. Naturally, rises in inflation have also been **taken into account**. Now, let me **break down** the figures for you all.

我們明年的預算期望能有如同去年的成長幅度。當然，通貨膨脹的增幅已納入考量了。現在，容我為各位分析數據。

Vocabulary

1. **one-off** [ˌwʌnˋɔf] *adj.* 一次性的
   New accounts are charged a one-off administrative fee.

2. **evaluate** [ɪˋvæljəˌwet] *v.* 評估
   It is the job of each manager to evaluate his own employees.

The first chart shows our current sources of revenue. As you can see, the majority of our funds continue to come from yearly membership fees. However, there has been an increase in **one-off**[1] visits. In fact, these now **make up** 16 percent of our revenue; whereas, 10 years ago, only 3 percent of our sales came from non-members.

Upon **evaluating**[2] this data, I'm **forecasting**[3] an even greater shift toward non-member purchases in upcoming years. This trend will continue until the economy is more stable and people feel comfortable paying for a year of gym fees **in advance**.

session [ˈsɛʃən] 指「（從事某項活動的）一段時間」。

Additionally, our month-long summer camp <u>sessions</u> have been giving us a much-needed **boost**[4] during the months when sales are historically lower.

Now, don't get too excited about these numbers yet. Next, I'll be going over our expenditures. Are there any questions before I move on?

第一張圖表顯示我們目前的營收來源。如你們所見，我們絕大部分的資金仍來自年度會費。然而，一次性的造訪數據有所成長。事實上，它們占了我們營收的 16%；而十年前，我們的營收僅 3% 來自於非會員。

在評估此數據時，我預測來年非會員的消費會有更大的轉變。這個趨勢將持續下去，直到經濟更穩定、大家願意花錢預付健身房的年費為止。

此外，我們為期一個月的夏令營活動，在銷售數據一向較低迷的月分中，帶出我們所需要的增長。

嗯，先不要為這些數據感到太興奮。接下來，我將說明支出的部分。在我繼續之前，是否有任何問題呢？

3. **forecast** [ˈfɔrˌkæst] v. 預測
Employers in the industrial sector are forecasted to take on thousands of new workers this fall.

4. **boost** [bust] n. 推動；促進
The tax cuts will give a welcome boost to the local economy.

簡報者接著針對預算支出做相關的
檢討與建議……

S = Speaker

S: Now that we've seen where our money comes from, let's take a closer look at how it's spent.

既然我們已了解收入來源,讓我們來細看是如何花費的。

> 讀做 [ˈɑbvɪəs],指「顯然的;明顯的」。

On this slide, it's <u>obvious</u> what's eating up most of our budget — new location openings. Here, you can see that almost 30 percent of our expenditures last year were directly related to the Morrison branch that was opened in Q3.

在這張投影片上,很明顯可看出是什麼占掉我們絕大部分的預算——開發新據點。從這裡大家可看到,去年近 30% 的經費和第三季開設的摩利森分部呈正相關。

Vocabulary

1. **trim** [trɪm] *v.* 縮減;削除
   The Neon Division is wasteful, and we need to trim its spending.

2. **cost-effective** [ˈkɔstəˈfɛktɪv] *adj.* 具成本效益的
   The CFO used cost-effective strategies to help increase profitability.

Bear in mind that the amount listed here does not include the costs of employee hiring or training for that location. All costs involving new personnel are born by HR. Obviously, an increase in locations is great for our **bottom line**, but we must find some way to **trim**[1] the budget in order to improve our net profits. This is why I mentioned the expense of hiring new employees.

讀做 [ˌdɪsprə`pɔrʃənətli]，指「不成比例地；不相稱地」。

According to this graph, our new hire costs have increased <u>disproportionately</u> to the number of positions in the company.

Basically, we are wasting time, energy, and money in the search for new staff because our employee retention rate is too low. It would be much more **cost-effective**[2] to find ways to hold on to our current employees longer. If each new hire remained an active employee for three years or more, it would **eliminate**[3] nearly 40 percent of HR's expenses. This is certainly something to think about.

I'd like to thank everyone for giving me their **undivided**[4] attention. I will now hand the floor over to Mike.

請記住，這裡所列出的金額不包括該據點的員工聘雇或訓練費用。和新進員工相關的所有支出都歸屬人資部。顯然地，新據點的增加對於我們的財務狀況是有幫助的，但我們也必須想辦法縮減預算以提高我們的淨利。這也是為何我提到招募新員工的支出。

根據這張圖表，新人招募成本的增加量與公司的職務量相比，實在不成比例。

基本上，由於我們的員工留職率太低，我們浪費了時間、精力和金錢在找尋新員工。找到方法來長留我們現有的員工，會更具成本效益。如果每個新進員工都在職三年以上，我們就能省下近 40% 的人資開銷。這當然是要考慮的事情。

感謝各位專心的聆聽。我將以下的時間交給麥克。

---

3. **eliminate** [ɪ`lɪməˌnet] *v.* 消除；排除
The tech department eliminated all the viruses on Dan's computer.

4. **undivided** [ˌʌndə`vaɪdəd] *adj.* 完整的；全部的
You must be prepared to give the job your undivided attention.

重點筆記

1. *take into account* 考慮；斟酌

說明	account [ə`kaʊnt] 指「估計；計算」，take into account 則是「把……計算在內；考慮」的意思，同義詞有 take account of、take into consideration 等。

- Jen doesn't eat meat, so take that into account before you cook dinner.
  珍不吃肉，所以你煮晚餐前要考慮到這一點。

- Before making a decision about whether to start a business, you need to take account of all the costs required for the initial investment.
  決定是否要創業以前，你得考慮初次投資所需的全數成本。

2. *break down* 分析

說明	片語動詞 break down 的常見用法如下：

Ⓐ 分析；分類（對話用法）

- The teacher broke down the long sentence into clauses.
  老師將這個長句分析成幾個子句。

Ⓑ 破壞；砸碎

- The police broke down the door to get in the house.
  警方將門破壞以進入屋內。

Ⓒ 拋錨；故障

- Michael's bike broke down after 10 years of use.
  麥克的腳踏車在用了十年後壞掉了。

Ⓓ 崩潰

- After her long exam, Hannah broke down and cried.
  經過漫長的考試，漢娜崩潰大哭。

3. *make up* 構成；組成

說明	片語動詞 make up 的常見用法如下：

Ⓐ 構成；組成（對話用法）

- These seven towns and their surrounding areas make up Denton County.
  這七個城鎮及其周圍區域構成了丹頓郡。

Ⓑ 編造（藉口、謊言等）

- Henry isn't really from Singapore. He just made that up.
  亨利並不是真的來自新加坡。他只是隨便編造的。

Ⓒ 和好；復合

- I had a fight with my friend, but we made up later that day.
  我和我朋友吵了一架，但是當天後來我們就和好了。

4. *in advance* 預先

說明	in advance 為副詞片語，有「事先；提前」的意思，相似拼法的 in advance of 則做介系詞，表示「在……之前；在……前面」，意思與 ahead of 類似。

- Peter asked his manager if he could be paid in advance.
  彼得問經理他能否預支薪水。

- Residents of the small town were evacuated in advance of the typhoon.
  這座小鎮的居民在颱風來襲前已撤離了。

5. *bottom line* 財務狀況

說明	bottom line 原本是財務報表位於「最末行」的數字，後引申指「結算盈餘或虧損」，即「財務狀況」之意。

- Cost cutting improved the company's bottom line.
  成本縮減改善了該公司的財務狀況。

6-2 Summing up Sales Figures
業績報告 I

業績起伏圖解詞典 &
簡報圖表實用句 PLAY ALL

業績起伏圖解詞典

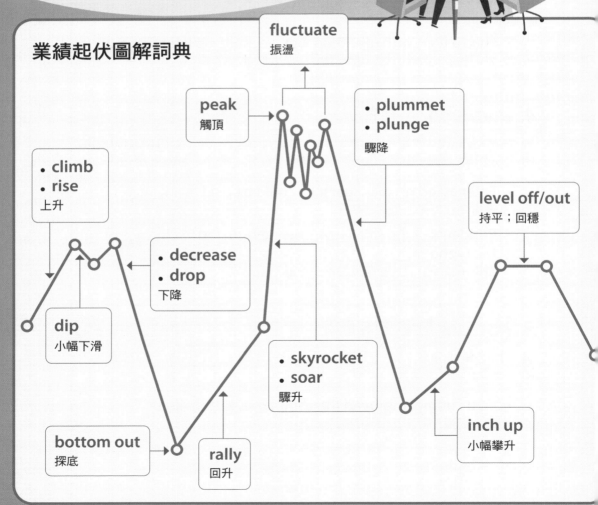

fluctuate 振盪

peak 觸頂

- plummet
- plunge
驟降

level off/out 持平；回穩

- climb
- rise
上升

- decrease
- drop
下降

dip 小幅下滑

- skyrocket
- soar
驟升

inch up 小幅攀升

bottom out 探底

rally 回升

簡報圖表實用句

Line Graphs 折線圖

- Our total sales have gone up/down for three consecutive months.
  我們的整體銷量已連續三個月成長／下滑。

- Profits from this product leveled off and remained stagnant for the next three months.
  這款產品的利潤趨於平穩，並在接下來三個月維持停滯狀態。

- In the 10th week, sales jumped sharply and hit a peak of 25,000 units.
  在第十週，銷量大幅躍升並衝到兩萬五千組的高峰。

Bar Charts 長條圖

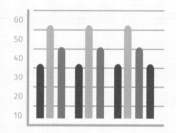

- Motor sales in Europe have seen a significant gain since last April.
  歐洲的汽車銷量從去年四月開始有明顯的增加。

- There has been a drastic drop in sales in the west region from last year.
  西區的銷量從去年開始急遽下降。

- Compared to last year, the south has shown great improvements.
  和去年相比，南區已有長足進展。

Pie Charts 圓餅圖

- This pie chart shows you our market share in the U.S.
  這張圓餅圖可讓各位了解我們在美國的市占率。

- Our current market share is 15 percent.
  我們目前的市占率是 15%。

- Our products make up around 12 percent of the shoe market in Taiwan.
  我們的產品約占台灣鞋類市場的 12%。

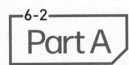
Part A 檢討銷售業績

史蒂夫（Steve）向莉莉安（Lillian）和馬丁（Martin）說明去年上半年的銷售成果……

S = Steve   L = Lillian   M = Martin

S: I'd like to begin by looking at the results for the first half of last year. This line graph <u>demonstrates</u> that we experienced dramatic fluctuations in sales during Q1.

> demonstrate [ˋdɛmən‚stret]
> 指「顯示；表明」。

我想從檢視去年上半年的成果開始。這張折線圖顯示我們在第一季經歷了銷售的劇烈波動。

L: Yes, that's quite apparent.* What were the reasons for this volatility?* Is this normal for that time of the year?

沒錯，是很明顯。造成如此波動的原因有哪些？這在一年當中的那個時間是正常的嗎？

Vocabulary

1. **consistent** [kənˋsɪstənt] *adj.* 穩定的
   Valerie has shown consistent improvement for years, so we are recommending her for a promotion.

2. **prompt** [prɑmpt] *v.* 促使
   One of our neighbors keeps dumping garbage in the street, which has prompted us to report him to the police.

S: To some extent. However, a lot of it was because of the downturn* in the economy. Looking at the graph, though, we can see that there was **consistent**[1] growth during Q2.

M: Still, it's disappointing that, **on the whole**, sales fell **beyond expectations** during that time.

S: I'd like to direct your attention to the next slide. In this graph, we can see sales picked up in the latter part of last year.

L: It's certainly reassuring* to see that sales climbed steadily from July to September. Why did they **level off** after that?

S: That's normal, Lillian. We offer a lot of back-to-school promotions in the summer to **prompt**[2] consumers to buy.

> 讀做 [spaɪk]，為名詞，
> 指「（統計圖表上的）暴增」。

M: I see there was a spike again in December. I assume that's **attributable**[3] to traditional Christmas buying.

S: You got it, Martin. That's precisely the reason.

某種程度上是。然而，絕大部分是經濟不景氣的緣故。不過從這張圖來看，我們可發現第二季有穩定的成長。

儘管如此，整體而言，銷量在那段期間的跌幅超出預期，還是讓人感到失望。

請兩位注意下一張投影片。在這張圖中，我們可看到銷量在去年下半年回升。

看到銷量從七月到九月穩步攀升，的確令人感到欣慰。為什麼之後就持平了？

莉莉安，那很正常的。夏季時，我們進行很多開學促銷活動來讓消費者掏腰包。

我看到銷量於十二月再次激增。我想那可歸因於傳統的聖誕節買氣。

你說對了，馬丁。正是這個原因。

---

3. **attributable** [əˋtrɪbjutəbəl]
   adj. 可歸因於……的
   The increase in emigration figures over the last few years is attributable to fewer job opportunities.

字彙補給站

* **apparent** [əˋpɛrənt] *adj.* 明顯的
* **volatility** [ˌvɑləˋtɪləti] *n.* 波動
* **downturn** [ˋdaʊnˌtɜn] *n.*（經濟）衰退
* **reassuring** [ˌriəˋʃʊrɪŋ] *adj.* 放心的

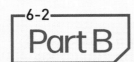

說明市占率

PLAY ALL • TRACK 56

馬丁接著向莉莉安和史蒂夫說明各
個分公司在上年度的銷售表現……

L = Lillian   M = Martin   S = Steve

L: Let's move on to **year-on-year**[1] performances of our international branches. Martin, can you **start** us **off**?

我們繼續來看國際分公司與去年同期相比的表現。馬丁，可以開始了嗎？

M: You can see from this bar chart that some branches have shown improvement. Others have experienced <u>declines</u> of up to 30 percent.

你們可從這張長條圖看到一些分公司已有進步。其他分公司的跌幅則達 30%。

decline [dɪ`klaɪn]
指「下降；減少」。

Vocabulary

1. **year-on-year** [ˌjɪrɑn`jɪr]
adj. 與上年同期數字相比的
Let's now discuss the year-on-year performances of our star products.

2. **sluggish** [`slʌgɪʃ] *adj.* 蕭條的
The housing market in this country has been very sluggish over the past few years.

252

L: I see the Spanish office saw **sluggish**[2] sales results compared to last year. How do you **account for** that?

我發現和去年相比，西班牙分公司的業績相當低迷。你要如何解釋這個情況？

M: The results are **in direct proportion to** our other European branches, actually. The drop is more **noticeable**[3] there because the sales volume is typically the largest. It **boils down to** a lack of consumer confidence in Europe.

事實上，這樣的結果和我們其他歐洲分公司成正比。那裡的跌幅更顯著的原因在於其銷量通常是最大的。這可歸結於歐洲的消費者信心不足。

L: At this point, I want to turn to a discussion of market share. Looking at this pie chart, you'll note there is <u>room for improvement</u>.

現在，我想轉往討論市占率。從這張圓餅圖來看，你們會注意到仍有進步的空間。

指「改進的餘地；進步的可能」。

S: That's certainly true. I had expected our share to rise.

的確如此。我原先預期我們的市占率會增加。

L: Me, too. Our current share of the market is 14 percent. Some of our competitors are standing much stronger with **upwards of** 20 percent.

我也是。我們目前的市占率是14%。我們的一些競爭對手表現更為強勁，市占上看 20%。

M: Yes, it seems that MegaMart has the biggest piece of the pie. It would be nice to **steal**[4] a bit of their market share.

是的，看來百萬商城的市占率最高。若能拿下一點他們的市占率會不錯。

S: The question is how. It's **easier said than done**.

問題在於要怎麼做。這說來容易做來難。

---

3. **noticeable** [ˋnotəsəbəl]
adj. 顯而易見的

There has been a noticeable improvement in the work that's been done since the new manager took over.

4. **steal** [stil] *v.* 巧取；竊取

The competing companies constantly tried to steal each other's customers.

重點筆記

1. *to some extent* 某種程度上

說明	extent [ɪkˋstɛnt] 指「程度；範圍」，可用 degree 替換。to some extent 即形容「達到某種程度」。若要表示程度的大小，則可寫成 to a large/great/small extent。

- To some extent, tourists are responsible for the damage to the hiking trail.
  某種程度上來說，遊客要為此登山步道遭到破壞負責。

- To a great extent, Ted owes his success to hard work.
  在很大程度上，泰德把他的成功歸功於勤奮努力。

2. *on the whole* 整體來看

說明	此片語形容考慮到所有的情況或條件，類似用法有 generally、in general。

- Reviews of the movie have been quite positive on the whole.
  這部電影的評論整體來看是相當正面的。

3. *beyond (one's) expectations* 超乎（某人的）期望

說明	expectation [ˌɛkˌspɛkˋteʃən] 指「期望；期待」，常用複數形，beyond (one's) expectations 即「超乎（某人的）期望」之意，反義說法則為 below (one's) expectations「不如原先所預期」。

- The expansion plan succeeded beyond all expectations.
  此拓展計畫的成功超出所有人的預期。

- The student was unhappy because the grade he received was below his expectations.
  這名學生不開心的原因是他的成績不如他原先所預期的。

4. *level off* （升或跌之後）趨於平穩

說明	level 當動詞指「使保持水平；使平坦」，level off 則用來表示數量或數字不再逐漸增加或減少，趨向平穩的狀態。

- After climbing to record highs, prices in the stock market started to level off and became stable last week.
  攀升至歷史高點後，股價於上週開始回穩並漸趨穩定。

5. *start off* 開始

說明	片語動詞 start off 的常見用法如下：

Ⓐ 使……開始（對話用法）

- Let's start off the meeting by introducing ourselves.
  我們從自我介紹來開始會議吧。

Ⓑ 從擔任……開始

- Jim started off as an office clerk and later became a manager.
  吉姆從公司職員開始做起，之後成為經理。

6. *account for* 說明

說明	account [əˋkaʊnt] 做不及物動詞時，常與 for 連用，有幾種意思：

Ⓐ 說明；解釋（對話用法）

- You need to account for all of the company money you spent during your business trip.
  你得就出差期間所花的全部公司經費做說明。

Ⓑ （在數量、比例上等）占……

- Sales of this product account for 80 percent of the company's income.
  此產品的銷售額占了該公司營收的八成。

7. *in direct proportion to . . .* 與……成正比

說明	proportion [prə`porʃən] 指「比例；比率」，常以 in direct proportion to 表示「與……成正比」，in inverse proportion to 則指「與……成反比」。

- The chef said that the quality of a dish increases in direct proportion to the freshness of its ingredients.
  主廚說一道菜的品質與食材的新鮮成正比增加。
- The money being spent on national security is in inverse proportion to that being spent on education.
  花在國家安全方面的經費與花在教育方面的成反比。

8. *boil down to* 歸結於

說明	boil [bɔɪl] 指「煮沸」，boil down to 則藉由字面義「透過煮沸的方式以蒸發水分」來比喻「歸結；簡化」。

- These problems boil down to two things — shortage of staff and lack of money.
  這些問題可歸結於兩件事──人力短缺與資金不足。

9. *upwards of* 超過；多於

說明	一般寫法為 upwards of，而 upward of 較為少見。此語之後接某數值，指「超過……」。類似用法有 in excess of、more than 等。

- The new Italian sports car cost upwards of NT$8 million.
  這輛新的義大利跑車售價超過新台幣八百萬元。

10. *easier said than done* 說來容易做來難

說明	此語形容某事物看似簡單，但執行起來卻非常困難，意近中文的「說來容易做來難」或「知易行難」。

- Passing that test next week will be easier said than done.
  通過下禮拜的考試是說來容易做來難啊。

延伸學習

說明業績數據

當數字遇上小數點

Ⓐ 小數點通常念成 **point**，小數點之前的數字為一般念法，小數點之後的數字可一個一個念（兩位數時亦可用十位數念法）。

> 例 **14.58** 讀做 **fourteen point five-eight** 或 **fourteen point fifty-eight**

> 例 **16.3451** 讀做 **sixteen point three-four-five-one** 或 **sixteen point thirty-four fifty-one**

Ⓑ 小數點後面數字為 5 時，有兩種說法：

> 例 **6.5** 讀做 **six point five** 或 **six and a half**

Ⓒ 數字為零點幾時：

> 例 **0.2** 讀做 **zero point two** 或 **point two**

說明數據實用句

Shares of Madison Square Garden, Inc., owner of the Knicks, rose 9.2 percent in five days.
尼克隊東家麥迪遜花園廣場公司的股價在五天內成長了 9.2%。

The price of gold fell 23.2 percent, nearly $400 an ounce, over the last year.
去年黃金的價格跌了 23.2%，幾乎來到每盎司四百美元。

Both companies have been performing well, but one brought in 5.9 percent more revenue than the other.
兩家公司的表現都很好，但其中一家帶來的營收比另一家多出 5.9%。

簡報圖表實用句 🔊 PLAY ALL

概要介紹

- You can see from the chart that **our sales to date have doubled since last year.**

  你們可從這張圖表看到我們目前的業績自去年已成長了兩倍。

- This graph shows **how our online sales have increased since the site launch.**

  這張圖表顯示我們的線上業績自網站推出後的增長情形。

- Looking at the chart, we can tell that **sales are down 25 percent year-over-year.**

  觀看這張圖表，我們可得知業績比去年同期下滑 25%。

折線圖

- Weekly sales for **the Upper West Side branch** hit a peak at **the end of August.**

  上西區分公司的週銷量於八月底達到高峰。

- **Our monthly recurring revenue** has leveled out and remains stagnant.

  我們的每月經常性收入已趨平穩並維持停滯狀態。

- Sales for **the southeast region** fluctuated wildly from **May** to **August.**

  東南區的業績從五月到八月呈現劇烈波動。

長條圖

- Our overall sales showed a 7 percent decline from the previous year.
  我們的整體業績比前一年下滑了 **7%**。

- There has been a year-on-year increase in **average deal size**.
  平均交易規模與去年同期相比是增加的。

- **The third quarter** showed no change in retail sales from the last one.
  第三季的零售業績與上一季相比沒有變化。

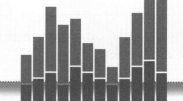

圓餅圖

- **Buster Inc.** has the biggest slice of the pie.
  博斯特公司的市占率居冠。

- We are standing strong with **25 percent of the market**.
  我們以 **25%** 的比率站穩市場。

- Our current share of the market is **9 percent**.
  我們目前的市占率是 **9%**。

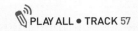 PLAY ALL • TRACK 57

Part A 報告整體業績表現

某糕點食品公司的業務經理潔西卡（Jessica）、業務協理布蘭登（Brendan）以及資深業務弗朗西斯科（Francisco）進行前三季的業績彙報。

B = Brendan   J = Jessica   F = Francisco

B: Why don't we take it from the start?

J: Right. As you can see from the graph, sales climbed steadily over weeks one, two, and three.

F: They leveled off briefly in week four and then **picked up steam** over the following seven weeks.

B: Was that around the time we **instituted**[1] our Lunar New Year promotion?

我們何不從頭說起？

好的。如你們從這張圖表所看到的，銷量在第一、第二及第三週穩定爬升。

銷量於第四週短暫持平，然後在接下來的七週加速成長。

那大約是我們展開農曆新年促銷的時候嗎？

Vocabulary

1. **institute** [ˈɪnstəˌtut] v. 開始；制定
   The firm instituted a flextime system to attract creative workers.

2. **hike** [haɪk] n. （價格或費用的大幅）提高
   Starting next year, the factory workers will receive a 15 percent pay hike.

3. **assessment** [əˈsɛsmənt] n. 評估
   We need a detailed assessment of the possible risks that we might run into.

J: Yes. Unfortunately by Q2, sales dipped noticeably.

是的。可惜到了第二季，銷量明顯下滑。

F: In fact, they plummeted from weeks 15 through 20, only to **bottom out** in week 21.

事實上，銷量從第十五週到第二十週驟降，在第二十一週達到最低點。

B: That's to be expected, though. The price **hike**[2] in material cost during <u>low season</u> **dealt us a** serious **blow**.

不過那是可預期的。淡季期間，原物料成本的價格調漲對我們造成極大的衝擊。

指「淡季」，相對的「旺季」則為 peak season。

J: That's our **assessment**,[3] too. The good news is once summer **rolled around**, sales skyrocketed. From our peak in early July through mid August, we were selling approximately 5,000 units a week.

那也正如我們所評估的。好消息是夏天一到，業績就一飛衝天。從七月初到八月中的旺季，我們一週大約有五千盒的銷量。

B: But that didn't **last**[4] for long.

但那並未持續太久。

F: No. **Irregular**[5] promotions and marketing <u>efforts</u> led to **erratic**[6] sales from the end of August through September. Fortunately, they've returned to normal levels and have remained stagnant since.

是沒有。不規律的促銷與不理想的行銷結果導致八月底到九月的銷量不穩。好在之後業績就回到正常水準並保持平穩。

effort [ˈɛfət] 於此指「（不理想的）結果」。

---

4. **last** [læst] *v.* 持續
   A consultation with our lawyer typically lasts 30 minutes.

5. **irregular** [ɪˈrɛgjələ] *adj.* 不規律的
   The doctor was worried about Susie's irregular heartbeat.

6. **erratic** [ɪˈrætɪk] *adj.* 不穩定的
   Markets remain erratic after the president announced new tariffs on foreign products.

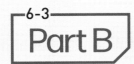 **Part B** 說明同期表現

接著，弗朗西斯科報告與去年同期相比的第三季業績。

B = Brendan   F = Francisco   J = Jessica

B: How does Q3 2019 **stack up** against Q3 2018?

2019 年第三季與 2018 年第三季相比的情況如何？

F: Looking at the bar chart, we can see strong retail sales led to a 20 percent <u>jump</u> in revenue from the previous year.

> 於此為名詞，指「激增；暴漲」。

觀看這張長條圖，我們可得知強勁的零售銷量使營收比前一年暴增 20%。

J: Our recently opened Xinyi and airport locations **posted**[1] especially impressive sales.

我們近期開幕的信義與機場店面公布了特別可觀的銷量。

Vocabulary

1. **post** [post] *v.* 公布（公司）財務結果
The manufacturer posted record profits from sales of its newest phone.

2. **rock-solid** [ˋrɑkˋsɑləd] *adj.* 非常穩固的
Iris was rewarded for her rock-solid performance with a generous bonus.

F: Yes, and while we experienced a 5 percent year-on-year decline in September, our **rock-solid**[2] showing in July and August more than **made up for** the slump.

是的，而雖然我們在九月歷經了 5% 的同期衰退，但七、八月的穩固表現多少彌補了此跌幅。

指「某人事物在競爭活動中的表現」。

讀做 [slʌmp]，指「（價格或銷售額的）暴跌」。

J: Marketing also played a **vital**[3] role. Their summer social media campaign proved to be very effective.

行銷部也扮演了相當重要的角色。他們的夏季社群媒體活動結果是成效卓著的。

prove [pruv] 指「結果是；證明是」。

B: In that case, both Sales and Marketing **deserve**[4] a big kudos.

那樣的話，業務部和行銷部都值得嘉許。

讀做 [ˋkuˏdos]，指「（隨某成就或地位而來的）聲譽、榮耀」。

---

3. **vital** [ˋvaɪt!] *adj.* 極其重要的
   A healthy diet, regular exercise, and quality sleep are vital for your health.

4. **deserve** [dɪˋzɝv] *v.* 值得
   Jan deserves all the credit for closing the deal with the fast food chain.

Part C　報告市場現況

最後，潔西卡報告公司的市占表現。

J = Jessica　　F = Francisco　　B = Brendan

J: I'd like to turn your attention* to the next slide. The figures here <u>show</u> our market share has grown from 8 to 16 percent over the period of a year.

我想將你們的注意力轉到下一張投影片。這裡的數字顯示我們的市占率在一年之間從 8% 成長到 16%。

解說圖表時，除了用 show，還有其他的動詞，一起來看看吧！
- depict [dɪ`pɪkt] 描述
- highlight [`haɪ‚laɪt] 強調
- illustrate [`ɪlə‚stret] 說明
- represent [‚rɛprɪ`sɛnt] 代表

Vocabulary

1. **ignore** [ɪg`nɔr] v. 忽略
   If we continue to ignore teens, we'll have a huge problem in the future.

2. **conduct** [kən`dʌkt] v. 執行；實施
   We conducted a survey to see if consumers are familiar with our products.

F: However, we remain in third place, and I feel this is because we've **ignored**[1] consumers' changing tastes.*

但我們依舊是第三名，而我認為這是因為我們忽略了消費者善變的口味。

J: I agree. We need to **branch out** and produce more than just pineapple cakes.

我同意。我們得擴展業務，不僅只是生產鳳梨酥而已。

> be open to + N./V-ing 指「願意……的；對……是接受的」。

B: Francisco, would you <u>be open to</u> **conducting**[2] some market research into the matter?*

弗朗西斯科，你願意針對這件事進行一些市調嗎？

> dig 原指「挖掘」，dig into 意指「往內挖」，在口語中喻指「挖探（消息）；深入探究（事物）」。

F: OK. I'll start by <u>digging into</u> what our competitors are offering.

好的。我會從競爭者所提供的產品開始研究。

B: Great. Now, I expect to see some superb* numbers as we move into Q4.

太好了。嗯，我期待在進入第四季時能看到一些漂亮的數字。

字彙補給站

❋ **attention** [əˋtɛnʃən] *n.* 注意力

❋ **taste** [test] *n.* 口味

❋ **matter** [ˋmætɚ] *n.* 事情

❋ **superb** [suˋpɚb] *adj.* 極棒的

重點筆記

1. *pick up steam* 漸漸活躍起來；漸有起色

說明	pick up 於此指「加速」，steam 指「蒸汽」，pick up steam 原形容蒸汽火車或蒸汽船等交通工具的動力逐漸增強，進而加速行駛，後引申指「逐漸開始發展；漸有起色」。

- Sales of the new product began to pick up steam at the beginning of the year.
  這款新產品的銷量在年初開始有起色。

2. *bottom out* 到達最低點

說明	此片語動詞形容某事物在不斷變化的情況下已達到最低點，並將開始獲得改善。

- Economists think that the recession in this country is bottoming out.
  經濟學家認為該國的經濟衰退將走出低谷。

3. *deal sb a blow* 打擊某人

說明	deal 指「予以……」，blow 指「重擊；打擊」，故整個片語形容「打擊某人；使某人受到挫折」。

- The scandal dealt the company a blow as its stock fell to record lows.
  這則醜聞重創了該公司，其股價也因而跌至歷史新低。

4. *roll around* （時間）到來

說明	動詞 roll 原指「滾動」，roll around 有「周而復始」之意，表示某時間或節日如往常般到來，同義詞有 come around。

- Bert can't wait for summer to roll around because he is going to Hawaii.
  柏特等不及夏天的到來，因為他要去夏威夷。

5. *stack up* 相比；匹敵

說明	stack up 原指「堆疊；累積」，後面加上介系詞 to 或 **against** 可表示「與……相比、匹敵」。

- The company's newest products don't stack up against the competition.
  該公司的最新商品無法與對手競爭。

6. *make up for* 彌補

說明	此片語指以某物「補償」已失去、損傷或缺乏的事物，如 make up for lost time「彌補失去的時間」。另一類似用法 make it up to sb 則指「補償某人」。

- The company's sales in Asia made up for its losses in Europe.
  該公司在亞洲的銷量彌補了其在歐洲的虧損。

- I'm sorry I missed your party last weekend, but I promise I'll make it up to you.
  很抱歉我錯過你上週末的派對，但我保證我會補償你的。

7. *branch out* 擴張；拓展

說明	branch 本來是「樹枝」，也可指「分支；分公司；支派」，當動詞則有「延伸；拓展」的意思，經常與副詞 out 連用。要表示「擴大經營範圍到某事物；涉足某個新領域」，可用 branch out into + N./V-ing 的句型。

- Our shop branched out from baked goods to coffee and sandwiches.
  我們的店面從販售烘烤食品擴展到販賣咖啡和三明治。

- The company sells clothing, but it has also branched out into food.
  該公司銷售服飾，但也拓展到食品業。

出版品預行編目資料

和全球做生意 必備簡報英語 / 陳豫弘總編輯 .

-- 初版 .-- 臺北市 : 希伯崙公司, 2020.09

面；　公分

ISBN 978-986-441-406-2（平裝）

1. 商業英文　2. 簡報　3. 讀本

805.18　　　　　　　　　　　109012400

《和全球做生意，必備簡報英語》讀者回函卡

謝謝您購買本書，請您填寫回函卡，提供您的寶貴建議。如果您願意收到 LiveABC 最新的出版資訊，請留下您的 e-mail，我們將寄送 e-DM 給您。

歡迎加入 LiveABC 互動英語粉絲團，天天互動學英語。請上 FB 搜尋「LiveABC 互動英語」，或是掃瞄 QR code。

姓名 ⬚⬚⬚⬚ 　**性別** □男 □女

出生日期 　年　月　日　　聯絡電話

E-mail 　
□ 我願意收到 LiveABC 出版資訊的 e-DM

學歷
□國中以下　□國中　　□高中
□大專及大學　□研究所

職業
□學生　　□資訊業　　□工　　□商
□服務業　□軍警公教　□自由業及專業
□其他

您以何種方式購得此書？
□書店　　□網路　　□其他＿＿＿＿＿

您覺得本書的價格？
□書名　□偏低　□合理　□偏高

您對本書的評價
	很滿意	還不錯	普通	不滿意	很後悔
書名	□	□	□	□	□
封面	□	□	□	□	□
內容	□	□	□	□	□
編排	□	□	□	□	□
紙張	□	□	□	□	□

您希望我們製作哪些學習主題？

您對我們的建議：

1 0 5

縣市

市區鄉鎮

村里路街

段

鄰巷

弄

號

樓

室

希伯崙股份有限公司客戶服務部 收

台北市松山區八德路三段32號12樓

英語數位學習第一品牌

電腦互動學習軟體 下載安裝說明

Step 1 請上網下載管理軟體（管理軟體僅須下載一次，如已下載請直接跳至 Step 3）

請至下方網站下載管理軟體，下載後執行安裝 (限 Windows 系統電腦安裝使用)。

http://ied.liveabc.com

點此下載

Step 2 下載完成後，請執行管理軟體

下載完成後點選執行檔即自動開啟管理軟體，並於桌面建立捷徑。

點選執行檔

LiveABC下載管理程式

安裝完成後可至桌面捷徑點選開啟

Step 3 開啟管理軟體後，登入下方卡片上的序號下載本書電腦互動學習軟體

請填入卡片上的序號，再按下確認，即可開始下載本書的電腦互動學習軟體。

下載中

電腦互動學習軟體下載序號卡

注意事項

• 次數限制：總共可安裝於 2 台電腦，共可下載安裝 6 次

電腦互動學習軟體
下載序號卡

一鍵下載隨時隨地學好語言
僅限使用於Windows系統

LiveABC
英語數位學習第一品牌

0550016

Step 4 執行電腦互動學習軟體，開始學習

① 下載後點選「管理及執行」

② 選擇學習書目

③ 按下執行開始學習

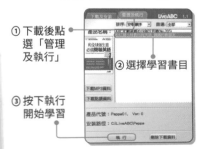